Laugh Lines

50 Years of Jokes, Stories, and Life as an Entertainer

Wayne Osmond

Sourced Media Books
San Clemente, California

For Mother and Kathy.
May 4 will always be my favorite day of the year.

Sourced Media Books
20 Via Cristobal
San Clemente, CA 92673
www.sourcedmediabooks.com

ISBN-13: 978-0-9841068-0-6

Printed in the United States of America.

This publication is designed to provide entertainment value and is sold with the understanding that the publisher is not engaged in rendering legal, accounting, or other professional advice. If legal advice or other expert assistance is required, the services of a competent professional person should be sought.

—From a Declaration of Principles jointly adopted by a
Committee of the American Bar Association and a
Committee of Publishers and Associations

Contents

Introduction

My mother, Olive Osmond, loved jokes. She loved telling them, hearing them, and even writing them. One of her favorite sayings was, "Tragedy plus time equals humor." Mother would often ask me to tell her jokes, so even as a child I began looking for them and collecting them. As I grew up, through the influence of my mother, looking for humor in different types of situations and even in unlikely places (a prison, for example!) became a permanent pastime.

Through the years, I have been fortunate to have traveled to many countries with different customs, languages, and types of humor. One thing I have learned is that while humor may differ depending on the region (try telling a Southern joke to a British person!), it is universal. Through humor, we are able to express happiness, relieve stress, make political commentary, and even assuage pain. Through humor, we are able to take ourselves a little less seriously and life a little less seriously, too. Humor can help us bring back perspective and forget some of the small stuff. That's why I love it and why I have spent a considerable part of my life collecting, using, and reusing jokes. (Anyone who has been to our Osmond Brothers concerts knows that I love to retell my favorites!) This book is my joke collection in its current form.

As we all know, some of the funniest moments come not from jokes but from life's messy situations. I have been asked by hundreds of people questions like, "What's it really like backstage?" "Are your brothers funny?" "Are you funny in real life?" and "What are your best memories?" I have some great stories about singing with Andy Williams, traveling in buses, rehearsing with my family, performing with animals, and many other situations that show business has a way of getting you into. I have also included some stories about me, written by my wife and children. Mostly, they're about how "unique" I am. I thought they were funny, so I threw them into the mix.

At the request of my family, I have included some other personal memories about myself, my brothers, my sister Marie, and my mother and father. I kept a diary growing up, so I included a few entries that shed light on life as a young entertainer, family dynamics, and the amazing strength and dedication of my parents. These stories and memories are interspersed throughout the book.

Finally, what's a book without pictures! In the book insert, you will find some of my all-time favorite pictures and captions that describe the event taking place.

Jokes, stories, memories, and pictures—an eclectic book, to be sure. I hope you will find it fun to read, and maybe you'll even find a new joke. Most importantly, I hope you'll search through your own family memories and find, as I have, a lifetime of laughs!

1

Animals and Insects

Over the years, I have worked with many different animals on stage. Who can forget Daisy, the pig who magically turned into a dancer every night in Branson? Though the Osmond Brothers have usually been the featured performers, there have been times when animals have taken center stage.

Many years ago, we were performing at a boat show. The opening act was a group of performing seals. They proved to be an extremely hard act to follow: not only was their performance flawless, but they got the stage really wet before our tap dance number. We slipped and slid across the stage in our tight, white pants and red jackets trimmed in white piping. But then it went from bad to worse. When the time came for my dance solo, I jumped up and did the splits in the air—and so did my pants. I ripped them from the front zipper all the way up the back to my waist.

The seals were the star performers of that evening, but nobody can steal a show like an elephant, especially an embarrassed one. When I was about 14 years old, we performed at John Asquaga's Nugget in Reno, Nevada. Our opening act was a pair of elephants, Bertha and Tina.

Poor Bertha got sick that day, and she dumped a big pile of elephant poo—center stage—right in front of the mike. The audience roared, but Bertha was a sensitive soul and was just plain embarrassed. So, she put her nose in the poo and started flinging it all over the audience! Many people left covered in dung from head to foot. The act was over for Bertha and Tina, and we were up next. Yep, another tap dance number. Alan, Merrill, Jay, and I came onto the stage, gulped, painted on a smile, and began the tumbling act—I mean tap dance. I slipped and fell. Enough said.

I've performed with a lot of animals, but my hands-down best performance ever was a private show: just me, my kids, and Alan's wife, Suzanne. One day, I was out in my garage tinkering around when my kids burst in screaming, "Dad! Dad! A snake!" I went into the front yard and there was a bull snake, coiled and hissing. I went into the safe in the garage, whipped out my .25 auto pistol, and shot it twice in the head. After I confirmed it was dead, I picked it up, looked around, and saw opportunity—Alan and Suzanne's house next door. With my train of kids following me, I knocked on the front door, and Suzanne answered. "Look, Suzanne!" was all I had to say before she was screaming and running wildly through the house. Of course, I ran after her with the snake, fueled by bursts of giggling and shouts of "Go Dad!" coming from behind. We had a pleasant race through her house and around her property. The look on her face was . . . priceless.

Jokes

What has four legs and one arm? A Rottweiler.

Why isn't there mouse-flavored cat food?

Would a fly that loses its wings be called a walk?

Why do they put bells on cows? Because their horns don't work.

Did you hear about the skunk that went to church? He sat in his own pew.

What do you get when you cross a pit bull with a collie? A dog that rips your leg off, then goes for help.

What did the mother buffalo say to her little boy when he went off to school? Bison.

Do you know why ducks don't fly upside down? They quack up.

What do you get from a pampered cow? Spoiled milk.

What do you get when you cross a snowman with a vampire? Frostbite.

What do you call a dog with no legs? It doesn't matter, he can't come anyway.

Where do you find a dog with no legs? Right where you left him.

What do you call three rabbits in a row, hopping backwards simultaneously? A receding hareline.

What do you call a fish with no eye? A fsh.

Yesterday I saw a chicken crossing the road. I asked it why. It told me it was none of my business.

Eagles may soar, but at least weasels don't get sucked into jet engines.

What do you call a cow with no legs? Ground beef.

What do you call a cow with two legs? Lean beef.

What do you call a cow that just had a baby? Decaf.

I went to see my horse the other day, and I said, "Why the long face?"

This man buys a pet parrot and brings him home. The parrot starts cursing him, using terrible language, and insulting his wife, so finally the man picks up the parrot and throws him in the freezer to teach him a lesson. He hears the parrot squawking and screaming in thére for a while, and then all of a sudden the parrot is quiet. So the man opens the freezer door, and the parrot walks out, looks up at him, and says, "I apologize for offending you, and I humbly ask your forgiveness." The man says, "Well, thank you, I forgive you." And the parrot says, "If you don't mind my asking, what did the chicken do?"

Two cows are lying in a field. One of them says to the other, "So, what do you think about this mad cow disease?" The other says, "What do I care? I'm a helicopter."

You can catch more flies with honey than with vinegar. But who wants a lot of flies?

The early bird would never catch the worm if the dumb worm slept late.

A lady opened her refrigerator only to see a rabbit inside. "What are you doing in there?" she asked. The rabbit replied, "This is a Westinghouse, isn't it? I'm westing!"

Two fleas meet in the street. One says to the other, "Do you want to walk or catch a dog?"

Turtles are helping science. Not long ago, the heart of a turtle was put into a man. The man walked out of that hospital one week later, and six weeks later he reached his car!

A camel can go five hundred miles without water. Science ought to find out how far it could go with water!

When we were on the 50th anniversary tour, we made a stop in Australia. So, naturally, Dad had to visit his friends at the local farm, namely the kangaroos, koalas, and wombats. Dad kept getting in trouble with our tour guide and his brothers for lagging behind the group. He had stashed kangaroo food in his coat pockets and kept feeding and talking to the llamas.

—*Michelle, Wayne's daughter*

A snake went to a psychiatrist and claimed that all of his friends kept sticking out their tongues at him.

His house was in such bad shape the termites ate out.

One fellow chased down a zebra and made a coat for his brother in jail!

A customer walked down the row of birds for sale in a pet shop. Passing one macaw, he heard the bird speak. The customer asked, "Hey, can you speak, stupid?" The bird replied, "You bet. Can you fly, dummy?"

A tomcat says to a female cat, "For you I would die." The female asks, "How many times?"

"Did you know it takes a half dozen sheep to make a sweater?"
"I didn't even know they could knit!"

A hunter hid in a tree so no one would take him for a deer. It worked. He was shot for a bear!

A young male octopus and a female octopus married in a sixteen-ring ceremony. Then they went through life hand in hand in hand in hand in hand in hand . . .

A baby porcupine says to a hairbrush, "Is that you, Mom?"

If a cow laughed, would milk come out her nose?

"My neighbor's dog bit me in the leg today."
"Did you put anything on it?"
"No, he liked it just as it was."

He called his dog Seiko. It was a watchdog!

My dog had worms, so the vet told me to feed it lots of garlic. Now its bark is worse than its bite!

A silkworm makes silk. A moth makes holes. I crossed the two of them, and now I have a bug that makes lace!

"What's the best thing for fleas?"
"Get them a nice dog!"

A lion complained to another animal, "I must be going crazy. Every time I roar, I have to sit through a movie!"

You can teach your dog to play fetch by tying your cat to a boomerang!

What did one cloned sheep say to the other? "I am ewe."

In 2008, our family celebrated the 25th anniversary of the Children's Miracle Network at Disneyworld. While we were there, we made a visit to the animal park. I enjoyed seeing the animals, but Wayne was in seventh heaven! We never made it over to visit the apes that day. He was so disappointed, he made me take a special trip back to the park with him the next day just to give the apes his regards.
—*Kathy, Wayne's wife*

A mother cat yelled at one of her kittens for coming home late. The kitten said, "Can't I lead one of my own lives?"

Fish must be brain food, because they travel in schools!

How much deeper would the ocean be without sponges?

May your liver never be mangled by a wild hippopotamus.

Old frogs never die . . . but they do croak.

The rooster may crow but the hen delivers.

What do cats like on a hot day? A mice cream cone.

What do you get when you cross a canary and a lawn mower? Shredded tweet.

What do you get when you cross a doorbell and a bumble bee? A real humdinger!

What goes "moof?" A cow with buck teeth.

What has four legs; is big, green, and furry; and if it fell out of a tree it would kill you? A pool table.

What has more lives than a cat? A frog. It croaks every night.

What insect does well in school? A spelling bee.

What is green and red and goes 1000 miles an hour? A frog in a blender.

Why do gorillas have big nostrils? Have you seen the size of their fingers?

Roses are red, violets are blue, horses that lose are made into glue.

What do you call a male ladybug?

What do you get when you cross a pig with a parrot? An animal that hogs the conversation.

What do you get when you cross a bull with a goose? An animal that honks before it runs you over.

What do you call a pig that does karate? A pork chop!

Do you know what goes zubb, zubb, zubb? A bumblebee flying backwards!

The woman I've been seeing says she eats like a bird. Birds consume four times their weight in food every day. I'll be dating a round robin in no time.

Why did the cat want to become a nurse? She wanted to be a first-aid kit!

What would you get if you crossed an electric eel with a sponge? Shock absorbers.

I spilled spot remover on my dog. He's gone.

Never pet a dog that's on fire.

Why do some dogs have flat noses? From chasing parked cars.

Dad loved dogs—labradors especially. We had a golden lab named Max and a black lab named Bear. Dad would borrow the neighbor's truck just to give our dogs the experience of riding in one. He loved to play with them and take them into the mountains with him when he went target shooting. Yes, Dad loved dogs. Except for Buddy.

Buddy was Alan and Suzanne's golden lab, and he was a frisky little guy that lived next door. He first got on Dad's bad side when he jumped up on my brother Steve (age 3) and scratched up his face. Then Buddy started knocking over our garbage cans and eating the dirty diapers. We waited until the last second to bring the garbage out to the truck, but Buddy often got to it, first—making our garbage look like confetti all over the cul-de-sac.

One day, Dad was fed up with Buddy. He had gotten into our yard and was making a mess, as usual. Dad decided to chase him out of the yard by shooting him in the rump with a pellet gun. It was meant to just sting a little; but the pellet was stronger than expected, and it lodged itself into the back of Buddy's hind quarters.

Dad immediately felt guilty for hurting Buddy. He picked him up, put him in our car, and took him to the vet, pampering him with the best medical treatment a dog could ever ask for. Buddy came home with a sore rump—and a new friend.

Dad and Buddy bonded over the incident and became good friends after that. They enjoyed playing frisbee and sharing funny stories about Alan. Buddy mostly listened.

—Michelle, Wayne's daughter

2

Bars

As a member of The Church of Jesus Christ of Latter-day Saints, I have made the commitment to abstain from alcohol. So, I don't have many personal stories under this section. To this day, I have never knowingly had an alcoholic beverage.

Now, you might wonder why I used the word "knowingly." One time we were performing at a fair in Peoria, Illinois with Bobby Rydell. My brothers and I were just kids at the time and were barely known on The Andy Williams Show. It was a humid, blistering-hot day, and those matching plaid blazers didn't breathe much. We were dying of thirst, so my father asked a guy if he would bring out a round of soda for us. A moment later, the guy came back with a tray of glasses.

"Father, something's wrong here," we said, after we took our first sips. My father took a taste.

"Yeah, wait a minute—don't drink that!" he said. Next, he tapped a woman on the shoulder and offered her one of the glasses. "Uh, lady, would you mind telling me what's in this glass?"

"Oh," she replied after taking a taste, "That's 7-Up and gin." As payment for her help, my father let her take the five full glasses of alcohol—free of charge. She was much obliged, not to mention a bit tipsy by the end of the show.

As members of the church, we also don't drink coffee. Naturally, I didn't know the first thing about making a cup of coffee, nor did I ever think I would need such a skill. But in the 1980s, I became a regular espresso service when I took a break from show business and flew jets professionally for the executives of Smith's Grocery Store. A man named Don Wittke, who turned out to be my best friend, gave me a job as his copilot. As part of my job description, it was my duty to make coffee for the passengers onboard. As you can imagine, I was not highly skilled at this but got to the point where I made excellent coffee. At least that's what everyone else said—I never tried it!

The effective delivery of bar jokes depends a lot upon the context in which the jokes are told—more so than for other types of jokes. They may be exceptionally funny at a bar or dinner club but not appropriate for other settings.

Jokes

A skeleton walks into a bar and says, "Give me a beer and a mop."

An anteater walks into a bar and says that he'd like a drink. "Okay," says the bartender. "How about a beer?" "No-o-o-o-o-o-o-o." "A martini?" "No-o-o-o-o-o-o-o." Finally, the bartender gets fed up and says, "Hey, buddy, if you don't mind me asking—why the long no's?"

What did the woman say to the drunk man sitting beside her? "Would you mind breathing the other way? You're bleaching my hair."

A pig walked into a bar, ordered fifteen beers, and drank them. The bartender asked, "Would you like to know where the bathroom is?" "No," said the little pig. "I'm the little pig that goes wee-wee-wee all the way home."

A man who has a little too much to drink staggers into an AA meeting. A member asks, "Are you here to join?" The drunk says, "No, I came in to resign!"

So this blonde walks into a bar and says, "Ouch. That hurt!"

A man walked into a big-city bar and looked around admiringly, saying, "This is a cute place, and I like the sawdust on the floor." The bartender said, "That's not sawdust. It's last night's furniture!"

That drunk man swallowed a boomerang. The bartender threw him out 28 times.

There's a $5.00 cover charge. When the shooting starts, they give you cover.

You look shiny and bright. Drinking Windex again?

What did the big chimney say to the small chimney? "You're too young to be smoking."

There's a new organization for people who want to give up drinking while they're driving. It's called the AA AAA!

3

Cars, Pedestrians, and Transportation

I've loved flying ever since I was sixteen. In fact, I got my pilot's license before my driver's license. Although many found it ironic that my mother had to drive me to the airport so I could fly myself around, I was completely content with this situation. Eventually, though, I figured out that it might be more efficient if I could drive myself to the airport. At age 18, I gave in and took a driving course—and flunked my driving test. The second time around went my way, and I've been driving ever since (much to my wife's dismay). One totaled car, 8 wrecks, and 15 tickets later, I'll admit I probably should have stuck with flying.

Though my driving record is admittedly bad, I've never let it get in the way of my mobility. I love taking the car out to run errands and to go exploring. My wife gets annoyed when I drive because I always want to take the creative path to get to a destination. (She wants to get there on time. Why, I don't know.) So, I save my expeditions for when she's not with me.

I've often found myself driving up into Utah's mountains where you can get away from the constant stresses of life. I equate the mountains with peace, and I've tried to instill this same feeling in my children. So, one beautiful Sunday afternoon, I took three of my kids (Steve, Greg, and Sarah) on a nice, quiet drive up Provo Canyon in my old, orange GMC Jimmy. We utilized the paved roads to a point, but then I decided to take us on a dirt path to really get a feel for solitude. It was absolutely beautiful up there, as we drove on windy paths next to sheer drop-offs. I don't think the kids appreciated it like I did—especially Sarah. Even as a three-year-old, she didn't trust me behind the wheel. She just cried, screamed, and said, "I want Mom!" as we dodged cliff ledges. But, the trip continued.

We were trying to go up and over a certain mountain, but we got to a point where the path was terminated by a five- or six-foot cliff. I had two options: make a tedious backtracking trek or drive the car straight off the cliff. I chose the latter. Being a responsible parent, I decided it would be best if my kids weren't in the car as I drove it off the cliff. I had them get out and stand off to the side of the trail—better view of the action from there, anyway. I backed the Jimmy up about 50 yards, put it in gear, floored it, and perfectly cleared the drop-off. I strapped the kids back in the car, and we were on our way. "See how relaxing the outdoors are, kids?" I apparently scared Sarah to death; to this day, she hates being in the car when I'm driving. I guess it's true that "the part of the car that causes the most accidents is the nut behind the wheel!"

One-liners like the above are best when accompanied by real-life examples. The next time you watch Jay Leno or Conan O'Brian crack a joke, analyze the joke's structure. It is usually a description of a situation accompanied by a snappy one-liner that pokes fun at the irony or absurdity of the story.

Jokes

What's the difference between a good pilot and a bad pilot? Well, a good pilot breaks ground and flies into the wind.

Remember, ride the subway during rush hour and you'll get your suit pressed for free.

What is the difference between a Harley and a Hoover? The location of the dirt bag.

The other day I stopped on a dime. Unfortunately, it was in a pedestrian's pocket!

Every problem can be solved except maybe how to refold a road map.

A juggler, driving to his next performance, is stopped by the police. "What are those knives doing in your car?" asks the officer. "I juggle them in my act," says the juggler. "Oh yeah?" says the cop. "let's see you do it." So the juggler starts tossing and juggling the knives. A guy driving by sees this and says, "Wow, am I glad I quit drinking. Look at the test they're making you do now!"

A wife told her husband, "Be an angel and let me drive." He did and he is!

I have a baby car. It goes everywhere with a rattle!

I know a fellow who put a beard on his Ford and told everybody it was a Lincoln!

The best way to stop the noise in your car is to let her drive.

A man in his beat-up old car drove up to a toll booth. The toll collector said, "Two dollars." The owner said, "Sold!"

I don't know how fast we were going, but the needle kept pointing toward my beneficiary!

Car service: If it ain't broke, we'll break it.

Drive defensively: Buy a tank.

Everything coming your way? You're in the wrong lane!

Fact: Red lights always last longer than green ones.

Humor is to life what shock absorbers are to an automobile.

Pedestrian: Someone who found a place to park.

There are two kinds of pedestrians: the quick and the dead.

I got pulled over by a policeman. I asked him for a warning so he fired three shots over my head.

His assignment was to blow up a car, but he burned his lips on the exhaust pipe.

Why did kamikaze pilots wear helmets?

The first time Dad let me drive a car was when he took me to Circus Circus in Las Vegas. On the way, he asked me if I wanted to drive. He put me on his lap and let me hold onto the steering wheel. Dad then pretended that he went to sleep. It freaked me out to think I was driving without any help, and I started crying. Dad then started chuckling, and I realized that he really was in control of the car.
—*Greg, Wayne's son*

He has the Midas touch; everything he touches turns into a muffler.

I asked my brother to check my turn signal to see if it was working. I turned it on. He said, "It's working. It's not working. It's working. It's not working. . . ."

A policeman spots a woman driving and knitting at the same time. Driving up beside her he shouts, "Pull over!" "No," she shouts back, "It's a scarf!"

Watch out! I drive like you do.

What is it about being alone in a car that makes people want to pick their noses?

He sent a limousine for me, but I got out of the way just in time.

A lady driving along hit a guy. She yelled, "Watch out!" He said, "Why? Are you coming back?"

Wife: I can't get the car started. I think it's flooded.
Husband: Where is it?
Wife: In the swimming pool.

Boy: You look prettier every minute. Do you know what that is a sign of?
Girl: Yes, you're about to run out of gas.

I had a weird dream last night. Dreamed I was a muffler. Woke up exhausted.

Did you hear about the guy who drove to Salt Lake City? He saw a sign that said, "SLC left," so he turned around and went home.

Did you hear that a big truck rolled on the freeway today? It was full of human hair and wigs. The police are still combing the area.

> When I was about five years old, my older brother Steve and I started arguing in the car. Dad was driving, and it was getting on his nerves; so, he pulled over, dropped us off by the side of the road, and told us to hold hands and walk home. We were sure that Dad was going to come back and get us, so we didn't dare let go of each other's hands or take a short cut. Well, Dad didn't come back to get us. But by the time we walked the mile home, we were laughing, talking, and the best of friends again.
>
> —Sarah, Wayne's daughter

I tried Flintstone vitamins once. They didn't make me feel any better, but I could stop the car with my feet.

I just bought a new car. I asked for a passenger-side airbag, and they gave me the salesman.

I had to stop driving my car for a while . . . the tires got dizzy.

A pedestrian is an object in the street that's invisible to drivers!

A pedestrian is a man who thought his wife gassed up the car!

Car sickness is the feeling you get when the monthly car payment is due.

A senator, a clergyman, and a Boy Scout were passengers in a small plane that developed engine trouble. We'll have to bail out," the pilot announced. "Unfortunately, there are only three parachutes. I have a wife and seven small children. My family needs me. I'm taking one of the parachutes." And he jumped.

"I'm the smartest politician in the world," said the senator. "The country needs me; I'm taking one of the parachutes." And he jumped.

"I've had a good life," said the clergyman to the Boy Scout, and yours is still ahead of you. You take the last parachute."

"Don't need to," shrugged the youth. "There are two parachutes left. The smartest politician in the world jumped with my knapsack."

Do you know, when a bug hits your windshield, what the last thing to go through his mind is? His hiney.

Two bugs hit the windshield and one bug says to the other, "I'll bet you don't have the guts to do that again."

Tailgater: One who makes ends meet.

Dad was a musician by night and a car mechanic by day. He had all the equipment in the garage—even a hoist—so he could fix his cars, himself. One of his tools measured exhaust fumes. On a routine checkup of his beloved orange Jimmy, he found that the carbon monoxide level was too high. He wanted to fix it, himself, but didn't have time. Rather, he bought three military-grade gas masks with goggles—the kind with the elephant trunks and the head gear. Whenever he took us for a ride in the Jimmy we had to wear the gas masks. Mom and Amy refused to ride, but Steve, Sarah, and I thought they were cool. We definitely got noticed driving down the street.

—*Greg, Wayne's son*

4

Computers, Inventions, and Technology

I've always been interested in technology and how things work. In fact, when I was a kid, I'd rip everything apart just to study and learn about the parts and how they fit together. I was also interested in electricity, electronics, and physics; and I read book after book because I thought it was so fascinating.

Electricity was one of my favorite things to learn about. My curiosity piqued when I was just three years old. One day, I was searching for some candy to eat. I finally spotted some, but it was above my reach. I found a nearby hamper that I used as a stepping stool. To stabilize myself, I grabbed onto the flue from the heater. There was a small lamp attached to the wall that had a short in the wire. It happened to be touching the flue, and current was flowing through it. When I touched the flue, I received an intense, painful shock that traveled all through my body. "What was that?!" I wondered. I've been hooked on electricity ever since.

Rigging alarms is another of my signature interests. When I was a teenager, someone was putting anonymous notes and flowers on my car every night. Naturally, I wanted to find out who it was. I rigged up an alarm by running two 60-foot wires from my condo out to my car and threading them through the engine so that they were properly concealed. I taped one wire to the window shield and the other to the window wiper. The idea was that when the anonymous gift-giver lifted the wiper to drop off the goods, the two wires would cross and complete the circuit. This would then sound an alarm that I had hooked up to speakers in my condo. At about three or four in the morning, the alarm sounded. I ran out to see who it was, but the person had vanished before I could catch her. Unfortunately, the alarm idea backfired, because that was the last time I received an anonymous note on my car.

My experiments with electricity and electronics have culminated in my never-ending search for sustainable power. I have been working on an invention in my garage for ten years, which my wife lovingly terms "the money pit" or "the flying saucer," depending on her mood. I have yet to get it to work, but I'm patient and tenacious.

Regardless of whether or not technology actually works, it makes for some great jokes that have broad audience appeal (just ask my kids how much mileage they've gotten out of jokes about my invention). Just be sure that your audience is young enough to know what you're talking about.

Jokes

Back up my hard drive? How do I put it in reverse?

To err is human. To really foul things up requires a computer.

The best part about computers is that they make very fast, accurate mistakes.

Do you know how you can tell that a blonde has been using your computer? There is white-out on the screen.

C:\DOS   C:\DOS\RUN   RUN\DOS\RUN

Why are men like blenders? You need one, but you're not quite sure why.

What is it called when a blonde blows in another blonde's ear? Data transfer.

An employee came home exhausted. His wife asked what had happened. The employee said, "Our computer went down, and I had to think all day!"

I have an electric toothbrush. Last month I forgot to pay my utility bill, so they came and turned off my teeth.

I have a new microwave TV set. I can watch a one-hour show in six minutes!

I'm not thrilled with all the gadgets in my house. It's scary having things around that are smarter than I am.

They just came out with a new kind of smoke detector. It has a snooze alarm.

The thermos is a great invention. How does it know when to keep things hot and when to keep them cold?

How about a frozen bandage for cold cuts?

We've just come up with a new anti-anti-anti-anti-missile. It has one drawback—it keeps shooting itself down!

The way they keep coming up with nuclear weapons, harp-playing may soon become a college course!

They now have a special Dial-a-Prayer number for atheists. You call it and nobody answers!

Alarm clock: A machine that scares the daylights into you.

Disinformation is not as good as datinformation.

Ethernet: Something used to catch the ether bunny.

Every time I hear the phone, it's ringing.

I haven't lost my mind. It's backed up on a disk somewhere.

It works better if you plug it in.

Maintenance-free: When it breaks, it can't be fixed.

If you make it idiot-proof, someone will make a better idiot.

Sufficiently advanced technology is indistinguishable from magic.

What did one magnet say to the other magnet? "I find you very attractive."

I got a shower radio for my birthday. Just what I need— music in the shower. I guess there's no better place to dance than on a slick surface near a glass door.

5

Funerals and Burials

Jokes about funerals and burials can be very funny, but they can also sting if you don't have the right crowd with the right sense of humor. Depending on the audience, a humorous anecdote or a well-placed joke can lighten the mood. For example, people from my church travel every week to the assisted living center in Bountiful, Utah to conduct church services for those who request them. At the assisted living center, it is not uncommon for a resident to pass on to the other side. But rather than dwell on the dying, the director of the center announces that someone has "graduated" from this life and gone onto the next. This subtle joke not only lightens the mood of the residents, but it also focuses on the fact that death is not the end; it is, in fact, just another step in life's journey.

This topic is particularly meaningful to me, since my mother and father have both recently passed away. I had the hardest time getting through my mother's funeral. When it was my turn to speak, I mentioned that I was my mother's favorite. Everyone thought that I was joking and started laughing. When I told everyone that I was serious, they started laughing even harder. You see, each of us feels we are our mother's favorite—but I really am!

My father's funeral was difficult for me, as well. I miss my father, George, because he was my flying buddy. My father always wanted to get his pilot's license. He even bought into a Piper Cub Airplane one time with the hopes of getting his own pilot's license but wasn't ever able to complete it; so I think I might have fulfilled that dream partially for him by becoming a pilot, myself. I miss the times that I used to fly my father to his ranch. We'd make about two trips per week from the Provo airport to the Logan airport and back. I look forward to the days when we will be able to fly through the skies together again.

Though I miss my parents a lot, I am comforted by the fact that we are still a family and I know I will see them again. In this context and with this perspective, funeral jokes are indeed funny. I'm sure Mother is on the other side laughing right along with me.

Jokes

Did you hear about the man who wrote the hokey pokey? He passed away. They had a hard time burying him. They'd put his left foot in and his right one would pop out—and he'd shake it all about.

She couldn't help throwing up at funerals. She was suffering from mourning sickness.

It is hard to understand how a cemetery raised its burial costs and blamed it on the high cost of living.

Remember this: Always go to the funerals of others, or they won't go to yours.

A man walks into a restaurant and says, "How do you prepare your chickens?" The cook says, "Nothing special, we just tell 'em they're gonna die."

The country game warden dies, and Sven and Ole devise a plan that will hopefully land one of them in the position. They flip a coin, and Ole calls it. "You'll be callin' the mayor, Sven," he says. So Sven calls up the mayor and says, "Mayor, I hear the game warden died last night. If it's all right with you, I'd like to take his place." The mayor replies, "It's all right with me if it's all right with the undertaker."

Hard work never killed anybody. But then, relaxing is responsible for very few casualties.

Eat right, exercise, and die anyway.

He's so dull, one day he was drowning and his entire life passed before him. He wasn't in it!

Why do they sterilize needles for lethal injections?

I get so upset when I see the obituary page. If you go by the photos, they all look so healthy!

One man I know tried to commit suicide a half-dozen times, but he gave up trying. It was ruining his health.

Suicide is the last thing a person should do!

Don't go into a mortuary that does cremating and ask, "What's cooking?"

There are two kinds of widows—bereaved and relieved.

A will is a dead giveaway.

Beware of dark rooms . . . they might be the morgue.

He's not dead, just electroencephalographically challenged.

What do you call a guy who's born in Columbus, grows up in Cleveland and then dies in Cincinnati? Dead.

What happens when you get scared half to death, twice?

This lady was riding on a bus and reading a statistics book on life expectancy. She turned to the man next to her and said, "Did you know that every time I breathe someone dies?" "Oh, really?" said the man, "That's interesting; have you ever tried mouthwash?"

I once saw a guy crying over this poor dead elephant at the circus. I said, "You must have been pretty fond of that elephant." He said, "I'm not. I have to bury it."

Now I know why they shoot people at sunrise. Who wants to live at five o'clock in the morning?

There was a man who took out a million-dollar life insurance policy. It didn't help; he died, anyway.

6

Dentists, Lawyers, and Other Occupations

Dentists are not the most popular people around. When it comes to professions, dentists are right up there (or down there) with lawyers and morticians! Why? Not only do they cause you pain, but you also have to sit there with your mouth hanging open for a couple of hours in a chair listening to "adult contemporary" elevator music!

My opinion of dentists changed, however, when my son Steve decided to pursue dentistry as a career. Steve is one of those people who was born to be a dentist. He was always an artistic child—at age eight, he sat on the front steps of our house and whittled clips for bolo ties out of balsa wood for hours on end. When he got older, he became interested in medicine but didn't want the long hours that went with it. He married a beautiful girl with beautiful teeth—whose dad was a dentist. And he had been told his whole life that he had an "Osmond smile," so he decided to use it to his advantage.

I knew he was really destined to become a dentist, though, when I saw the pleasure he took in brushing his children's teeth. One night, he was over at our house with his family and began to get the kids ready for bed. His oldest daughter was about two at the time, and she had a stubborn streak about the size of his. Steve's daughter was not interested in brushing her teeth, so Steve took matters into his own hands. Steve put her on his lap and happily brushed her teeth for a full two minutes while she kicked and screamed and tried to bite. When the two minutes were up, she trotted happily off to bed, and Steve said with a smile, "Got to brush those teeth." Some call that act of service being a dedicated father, but we knew from the look of satisfaction on his face that he took intrinsic pleasure in brushing people's teeth—whether they liked it or not.

So Steve, this chapter is for you. I hope you can use some of these jokes on your patients (the ones you used on me were pretty good, but you can always expand your repertoire). A captive audience is often the best kind, and yours will be looking for any kind of relief!

Jokes

What do you have when you've got six lawyers buried up to their necks in sand? Not enough sand.

Why does New Jersey have so many toxic waste dumps and Washington, D.C. have so many lawyers? New Jersey got first choice.

The judge said to his dentist, "Pull my tooth, the whole tooth, and nothing but the tooth."

What did the lawyer name his daughter? Sue.

I like political jokes unless they get elected.

A barber was shaving a customer. About ten strokes in, the barber asked, "Did you have ketchup for lunch?" The customer answered, "I haven't had lunch." "Well, then," the barber said. "I think I cut your throat!"

The barber was far from proficient, nicking the customer more than once with his sharp razor. After the shave, the customer asked for some water. "Are you thirsty?" the barber asked. "No. I just want to see if my face leaks!"

A barber cuts a man while shaving him. To assuage the man's anger, the barber says, "Can I wrap your face in a hot towel?" The man says, "No. I'll just carry it home under my arm!"

My barber isn't the best. When I go in for a shave, I ask for ether!

"Your hair is getting gray."
"Try cutting a little faster!"

I know why they call it a crewcut. It looks as if it was cut with an oar!

My barber is so bad he cuts himself with a towel!

If you've ever been shaved in a barbershop, you're sure to have wondered why they call Santa Claus "Saint Nick!"

Samson must have had the right idea about advertising. He took two columns and brought down the house.

One advertisement in magazines doesn't make sense. It tells you to take a certain laxative and stay in bed!

It was a brilliant idea to make army fatigues and army food the same color!

The army jacket they issued to me was so long it came with shoelaces!

"How does your new uniform fit, soldier?"
"The coat is fine, but the pants are a little loose around the armpits!"

Everything issued was olive drab. One soldier fainted on the barracks lawn and they didn't find him for two days!

A new recruit couldn't understand why they called him "Private." He slept in a room with eighty other guys!

How can they advertise that certain headache tablets can give relief in seconds, when it takes an hour to get out the cotton?

"Beg pardon, General, but the troops are revolting." "Well, Captain, you're pretty repulsive, yourself!"

My attorney is brilliant. He didn't bother graduating from law school. He settled out of class!

Coming out of a restaurant, a man met his dentist on the way in. The man asked, "Listen, what should I do about my yellow teeth?" The dentist said, "Wear brown."

A dentist was working on a young woman patient and kept telling her to open her mouth wider and wider. Finally she asked, "Aren't you planning to stand outside?"

He goes to the dentist twice a year—once for each tooth!

Happiness is listening to your dentist promise that it won't hurt, then watching him stick himself with a drill.

An efficiency expert is a man who's smart enough to tell you how to operate your business—and too smart to start one of his own.

An expert is somebody who learns more and more about less and less.

She's a housekeeper. Every time she gets divorced, she keeps the house.

My dentist just put in a tooth to match my other teeth. It has three cavities!

I was going to be an astrologer, but I couldn't see a future in it.

The plumber came up from examining the damage and said, "Your basement has a bad leak. Should I fix it, or do you want to pretend you live in Venice?"

The plumber asked the lady of the house, "Where's the drip?" She answered, "He's in the basement trying to fix the leak!"

He went crazy because of the job he had. He took out the garbage in a boomerang factory.

A policeman stopped a lady for speeding. The lady said, "I wasn't doing ninety." The policeman said, "I'm going to give you a ticket for trying!"

Wayne's Diary

Friday, Aug. 12, 1966

Huntsville, Utah

Dear Diary,

Today we got up and left for the dentist's office. Alan was first, then, it was my turn. I had six cavities in two teeth! I have to go back again on the 16th. Later I went with mother shopping; then, we went to a health store. We had a yogurt sundae and some carrot juice with coconut milk in it. Boy! It sure was good! We did a little more shopping and my tooth was really hurting by now. We went back to the dentist's office, [then] I ate seven peanut butter and jam sandwiches! I played my clarinet and I've almost got "12th Street Rag" learned! I watched the 10:00 o'clock news and went to bed.

The town elected a new police chief. His first job was to arrest the old police chief.

A cop walked over to a man in a stalled car and said, "What's the matter with you?" The man said, "Nothing. I had a cold last week, but now I'm fine."

One candidate was so dull, there was a rumor he'd had a charisma bypass!

Our last mayor did the work of two men—the James brothers!

Most politicians don't believe a word of what they say. They're surprised that we do!

He's just the man to get our town moving. If he wins, I'm moving!

A man applied for a job and was asked to tell about his work experience. He said, "From time to time I was a door-to-door salesman selling wall-to-wall carpeting on a day-to-day basis with a 50-50 commission in Walla Walla." "How was business?" the interviewer asked. "So-so."

One salesman said that he'd gotten three orders that week—get out, stay out, and don't come back!

The boss said, "You must answer the phone when it rings." The secretary said, "Most of the time it's for you!"

A woman was bathing when there was a knock on the door. From the other side, a man said, "Blind man!" Because she was charitable, the woman got out of the tub and, without bothering to put on her robe, walked to the door and opened it. The man said, "All right, lady. Where do you want me to put the blinds?"

A nearsighted dentist passed a xylophone and said, "Your folks ought to bring you in for braces!"

Confession is good for the soul but bad for the career.

Electricians don't wear shorts. They just fix them.

Help wanted: Telepath. You know where to apply.

Honk if you love peace and quiet.

I'm a corporate executive—I keep things from happening.

Pilots are just plane folks.

Postmen never die, they just lose their zip.

Sign seen in a veterinarian's office: The doctor is in. Sit. Stay.

Did you hear about the butcher who accidentally backed into the meat grinder? He got a little behind in his work.

Did you hear about the dentist who married a manicurist? They fight tooth and nail!

What do you call a crazy baker? A dough nut.

What do you call a drunk who works in an upholstery shop? A recovering alcoholic.

What do you call a veterinarian with laryngitis? A hoarse doctor.

What is a chimney sweep's most common ailment? The flue.

Our company's dental plan is "chew on the other side."

"Bald Is Beautiful Convention" in Moorhead, SC.

"Plastic Surgeons Convention" in Scarsdale, New York.

"Psychiatrists Convention" in Normal, Illinois.

"Accountants Convention" in Billings, Montana.

"Mystery Writers Convention" in Erie, Pennsylvania.

"Weight Watchers Convention" in Gainesville, Florida.

"Contortionists Convention" in Southbend, Indiana.

"Plumbers Convention" in Flushing, New York.

"Lawyers Convention" in Sioux City, Iowa.

He has meant to his profession what waterskiing has meant to the economy of Arizona.

What looks good on an attorney? A Doberman.

Then there is the dentist who complimented the hockey player on his nice, even teeth: one, three, five, seven, and nine were missing.

Why do they call it "politics?" From the Latin, *poli*, meaning "many," and *tics*, meaning "bloodsucking parasites."

What's the difference between a trampoline and a lawyer? You take your shoes off to jump on a trampoline.

I had a boring job. I cleaned the windows in envelopes.

How many people work here? About half of them.

If we quit voting, will they all go away?

One day a man spotted a lamp by the roadside. He picked it up, rubbed it vigorously, and a genie appeared. "I'll grant you your fondest wish," the genie said. The man thought for a moment, then said, "I want a spectacular job—a job that no man has ever succeeded at or has ever attempted to do." "Poof!" said the genie. "You're a homemaker."

If the cops arrest a mime, do they tell her that she has the right to remain silent?

A little girl asked her father, "Daddy, do all fairy tales begin with "once upon a time?" He replied, "No, there are a whole bunch of fairy tales that begin with, "If elected, I promise."

Did you hear about the gardener who refused to work without his favorite shovel? "I never heave loam without it."

I told him to go out and get a job so we can see what kind of work he's out of.

"What does G.M.T.C.B.C. stand for on your business card?" "Give me the card back, chubby."

"Why don't you come to work on time?" "Because it makes such a long day."

He was a waiter in an insane asylum. He served soup to nuts.

Why do they call it "rush hour" when nothing moves?

Law firm: Dooey, Cheatum, and Howe.

Stockbroker: Eeny, Meeny Miny, and Moe.

In the Olympics, he was a javelin catcher.

Ask not what the government can do for you. Ask what the government is doing to you.

The Selective Service isn't very selective; they take everybody.

His success is due to long hours, hard work, and total disregard for quality.

Police station toilet stolen. Cops have nothing to go on.

Do Roman paramedics referer to IV's as "4's"?

On my 21st birthday, Mom and Dad took me out to dinner at Applebee's. When we walked in, Dad greeted the server and quickly noticed her multiple ear piercings. Dad would never hurt anyone's feelings on purpose, but he couldn't resist telling an old joke. He said to the server, "You look like you fell into a tackle box." I don't think the server knew what Dad was talking about, which was good. As we sat down to eat, Mom and I told Dad that his comment was a little offensive. Dad felt so badly that he apologized to the server three or four times.

—*Michelle, Wayne's daughter*

7

Doctors and Illness

Life is wonderful, but sometimes it's tough; and when the hard times come, you either have to laugh or cry about them. I've tried to laugh, and my family has helped me all the way. For example, when I was in the hospital recovering from brain surgery, my sister Marie sent me a balloon every day with a joke tied to the string. Those jokes (and the morphine) really helped. And when I was finishing my radiation treatments, my brother Jimmy actually left his family for an entire week to help me get through it. He and his arsenal of toys gave me the strength to finish the treatments and recover quickly. (We would shoot foam darts at the TV for hours!) Thanks, Jim.

I'll admit the hospital stay wasn't my favorite time of life, but I appreciated and admired the doctors that were able to cure my cancer. I always wanted to go to medical school, and I imagine that I would have become a doctor if I hadn't been in show business. The lack of a medical degree never stopped me from practicing medicine, however. I always try to fix all of my family members' ailments. I have doctored everything from broken toes and ingrown toenails to back problems. Sometimes my remedies work . . . and sometimes they don't.

Right before Kathy and I got married, she was concerned because she had a bit of acne on her face. I knew the perfect remedy. I owned a gizmo called "the electric rake" that used electricity to clear out hair follicles and regrow hair. I was convinced that if I used it on Kathy's skin, the electricity would zap the pimples and then give Kathy the ultra-clear skin that she wanted for our wedding day. Well, I zapped her skin; but instead of obliterating the pimples, I coaxed them to the surface. Sorry about that one, Kathy. Luckily, I did it early enough before the wedding that the pimples went away on their own.

Though I never became a doctor, my dreams of having a doctor in the family were fulfilled when my son Greg graduated from Duke Medical School this year. Greg may have gotten the diploma, but I have pictures wearing his graduation cap and gown. So I get to wear the cap and gown, and he gets to do all the work. Sounds good to me.

Telling doctor jokes is a surefire way to get a laugh from a crowd, because we all identify with them. Who hasn't been to a quack doctor? (My daughter Amy once went to a gynecologist who told her that dairy farmers were the real experts on lady problems.) These may not be the best jokes to tell if you're the keynote speaker for the AMA. But then again, they may.

Jokes

"Doctor, doctor, I've only got fifty seconds to live."
"Come in and sit down for a minute."

"Doctor, doctor, every time I drink a cup of hot chocolate I get a pain in my right eye."
"Try taking the spoon out of the cup, first."

I bought a self-help video called, "How to handle disappointment." When I got it home, the box was empty.

I told my doctor I had shingles. He tried to sell me vinyl siding.

Whenever I feel blue, I start breathing again.

I told the doctor I have a trick knee. "What should I do?" I asked. He said, "Join the circus."

I asked my doctor if it was serious. He said, "Only if you have plans for next year."

My doctor came in to see me. He said, "Your tests are back. Don't come any closer."

I said to my doctor, "I want a second opinion." He said, "Sure, as soon as you pay for the first one."

Doctors can be frustrating. You wait a month-and-a-half for an appointment, and they say, "I wish you'd come to me sooner."

We were so poor that we couldn't afford x-rays, so the doctor would just hold us up to the light.

I went to the doctor the other day. I said, "Doc, I can't sleep. One night I dream I'm a wigwam. The next night I dream I'm a Tepee." He said, "That's easy. You're two tents (too tense)."

I went to the doctor the other day, and I said, "Doc, what's wrong with me? I wake up in the morning, I look in the mirror, and I just wanna throw up!" He says, "Well, I don't know, but your eyesight's perfect."

I'd like to sing a solo. "Born free. My father's a doctor."

I went to the doctor and said, "Doc, I have a problem with my eyes." "Have they ever been checked?" he asked. "No, they've always been brown."

I told my doctor, "Doc, I think I'm going to die"; so he made me pay in advance.

"I have terrible news, Mr. Larson. You have cancer and you have Alzheimer's."
"Well, Doc, at least I don't have cancer."

"Doctor, Doctor, I have a problem. I'm shrinking."
"You'll have to be a little patient."

"Doctor, am I going to die?"
"That's the last thing you're going to do."

"Doctor, I feel like a pair of curtains."
"Come now, pull yourself together."

My dad is a very handy person. He has every tool imaginable and can tell you how to fix anything. One of his favorite projects was finishing the basement of our house in Provo, Utah. He did the wiring, plumbing, sheetrock, trim—I mean, all of it. I used to follow him around wearing my matching tool belt with a miniature hammer and tools, just like him.

One day when I was going out to catch the carpool for school, I was startled by a stranger in the garage looking through our garbage cans. I was about to yell out to call 911 when the stranger called out, "Steven." I then realized that it was my Dad, looking like a mummy, with a white bandage wrapped around his head. Then he began to tell me the story of the night before, when he fell off of a ladder and sliced off part of his ear. I felt so badly until Dad starting laughing hysterically. I guess a sense of humor really does fix anything.

—Steve, Wayne's son

"Mrs. Brown, you're not going deaf in your left ear. You seem to have a suppository stuck in there!"
"Well, now I know what happened to my hearing aid."

I almost got killed twice today. Once would have been enough!

"Doctor, I don't know what's wrong with me, but I hurt all over. If I touch my shoulder here, it hurts, and if I touch my leg here, it hurts, and if I touch my head here, it hurts, and if I touch my foot here, it hurts."
"I believe you've broken your finger."

The doctor calls up the patient and says, "I have some bad news and some worse news. The bad news is that you have only twenty-four hours left to live." And the patient says, "That is very bad news. What could be worse than that?" The doctor says, "I've been trying to reach you since yesterday."

Doctor: I'm afraid I have some bad news. You're dying and you don't have much time.
Patient: Oh no! How long have I got?
Doctor: Ten . . .
Patient: Ten? Ten what? Months? Weeks?
Doctor: Nine, eight, seven, six . . .

"What happened to you, Mr. Jones? You look awful."
"Well, Doctor, you told me to take this medicine for three days and then skip a day, and all that skipping wore me out."

Patient: Nurse, I keep seeing spots in front of my eyes.
Nurse: Have you ever seen a doctor?
Patient: No, just spots.

Patient: Doctor, you've got to help me. Some mornings I wake up and think I'm Donald Duck;

other mornings I think I'm Mickey Mouse.

Doctor: Hmm, and how long have you been having these Disney spells?

A Japanese visitor went to an American eye doctor. After an examination the doctor said, "You have a cataract." The Japanese visitor shook his head. "Oh no! I have a Rincoln Continento!"

A man was brought into the emergency room at the local hospital. He had drunk from a bottle marked "poison." The physician asked, "Why would you drink from a bottle marked 'poison'?" The man answered, "Underneath, it said 'lye,' so I didn't believe it!"

August 18, 1966; Huntsville, Utah

A [dirt] clod slipped out from under my foot and one of those metal fence posts caught my leg just above the knee tearing it 4 inches long and ³/₄ inches deep as I fell in the water. . . . Father got his keys and he, Alan and I left for the Dee hospital. We got behind a few slow drivers but we finally got there. The nurses came out with a wheelchair, and I went into the emergency room. . . . After, the nurses washed it and cleaned it. The doctor gave me 19 shots of novocaine and I had better than 40 stitches! I also had to have a Tetanus shot. I was just figuring. The two times I was at the dentist's office and today at the hospital I've had 42 shots! . . . We went home and everybody fussed over me. . . . Then I went to sleep again.

P.S. Before Mother came she told me the family had prayer for me and Virl said it.

P.P.S. I've got the best family in the world.

Patient: What's wrong? Why am I in a hospital?
Doctor: You've had an accident.
Patient: What happened?
Doctor: Well, I've got some good news and some bad news.
Patient: What's the bad news?
Doctor: We had to amputate both of your legs.
Patient: Oh no! What's the good news?
Doctor: We found a guy who's made a very good offer on your shoes.

"Doc, what do I do for a broken leg?"
"Limp!"

Olive Osmond

In 1966-67 George, Alan, Wayne, Merrill and Jay had just returned from their first trip to Sweden. We were living in Huntsville. They had all bought a nice camera. Alan had a Hasseblad and was so careful with it.

Wayne was down by the pond looking around when all of a sudden he cried out for help. Alan heard him and knew something was seriously wrong. He jerked the camera from around his neck, laid it quickly on the ground and dashed to help Wayne. He had gashed his leg severely on a metal post that was sticking up out of the ground and had to be taken to the hospital immediately where he had lots of stitches.

A doctor examined a man and said, "I don't like the looks of him." The man's wife said, "I know, but he's so good to the children."

Then there's the unethical allergist. He keeps a dead cat in his desk drawer!

"Mrs. Klein, your husband will never be able to work again." "I'll tell him. That'll cheer him up!"

The patient came into the doctor's office, suffering from amnesia. The doctor asked, "Have you ever had it before?"

A woman rushes into a doctor's office and says, "Doctor, what should I take when I'm run down?" The doctor says, "The license number."

A man rushes into a drugstore and says, "Do you have a cure for hiccups?" Without warning, the druggist hits him in the face. The man says, "What the heck are you doing?" "You don't have the hiccups now," the druggist says. "No, but my wife out in the car does!"

Insomnia is the triumph of mind over mattress!

A patient spent three hours in the doctor's office waiting to be examined. Finally he called it quits and went home to die of natural causes.

A man comes into a drugstore and says, "I want some acetyl salicylic acid." The druggist says, "You mean aspirin?" The man says, "I can never remember that word!"

The doctor told me that he'd have me on my feet in no time. It was true. I had to sell my car to pay his bill!

It was a wonderful hospital—Our Lady of Malpractice.

We called in a tree doctor, but he fell out of his patient!

"I just came back from my doctor."
"Which doctor?"
"He's been called worse!"

He bled so much after his fights that the Red Cross would siphon up the canvas!

My doctor told me to play thirty-six holes a day, so I went out and bought a harmonica.

I've had a lot of antibiotics, lately. When I sneeze, I cure somebody!

I wouldn't allow my surgeon to use a local anesthetic. I can afford something foreign!

This surgeon told his patient, "I have bad news and good news for you. The bad news is—I cut off the wrong leg. The good news is—your bad leg is getting better!"

The hospital food was so bad I begged them to put me back on intravenous feeding!

Something has to be wrong—we spend sixty million a year on medical research, two billion a year on medical care, and two billion on get-well cards.

"What can I do for insomnia?"
"Pretend you're a night watchman!"

I finally got a night's sleep last night, but it didn't do me a bit of good. I dreamed I was awake all night!

"Doctor, my arm got broken in two places."
"Don't go back to either of them!"

One poor soul drowned from smoking. He burned a hole in his waterbed and fell in!

In a hospital today there's lots of TLC—Take Lotsa Cash!

Did you know that diarrhea is hereditary? It runs in your jeans.

Diplomacy: The art of letting someone have your way.

Diplomacy is the art of saying 'nice doggy' until you can find a rock.

Does your back go out more than you do?

Feeling good? Don't worry, you'll get over it.

"Hello, operator. This is an emergency! What's the number for 911?"

NyQuil: The stuffy, sneezy, why the heck is the room spinning medicine.

The colder the x-ray table, the more of your body is required on it.

Dad had a medical procedure done a few years ago, resulting in 15 staples in his head. They were itching, and he was determined to take them out even though his doctor's appointment was still two days away. So he solicited my help. "Sarah," he said. "I can't stand these staples one second longer. You're a CNA. You take them out." I protested that I wasn't his doctor and didn't have the right medical equipment, but he insisted. "Just yank them out," he said. I had no choice but to grab a pair of tweezers and carefully remove them: it was either him or me, and I didn't want those staples pulled out by his Snap-On pliers!

—*Sarah, Wayne's daughter*

Time flies . . . when you're in a coma!

Dain bramaged.

Remember, germs are carried in the air; so avoid breathing air unless you know where it's been.

I said, "Doc, my nose is sore." He said, "Stay off of it for a couple of weeks."

When I had my last surgery they left a sponge in me. I don't have any pain but now I get real thirsty.

"Doc, how do I stand?" He said, "That's what I'd like to know."

The next time you go to the hospital make sure you are fully covered by your insurance and your gown.

Doctor: Our testing shows you're clearly schizo-phrenic. You have twin personalities.

Patient: Yes, one of me sees that clearly. But the other me wants a second opinion.

The patient's family gathered to hear what the specialists had to say. "Things don't look good. The only chance is a brain transplant. This is, however, an experimental procedure. It might work, but the bad news is that brains are very expensive, and you will have to pay the costs yourselves."

"Well, how much does a brain cost?" asked the relatives.

Then the patient's daughter asked, "Why is there a difference in price between male brains and female brains?"

"A standard pricing practice," said the head of the team. "Women's brains have to be marked down because they're used."

"Doc, I think I'm losing my memory."
"How long have you had this problem?"
"What problem?"

"Doc, I have a cold or something in my head." He said, "I'll bet it's a cold."

Never let a plastic surgeon get near a fire. They melt.

Doctor: How did you get here so fast?
Patient: Flu.

Do you know what cosmetic surgery you never hear about? Nose enlargement.

A husband was troubled that his wife was experiencing some hearing loss so he sought the advice of a physician. The doctor suggested a simple test to determine if, indeed, there was a problem. When the fellow returned home that evening, his wife was preparing dinner at the stove.

"Hi, dear," he said in a normal tone of voice. "What's for dinner?" No answer. He took a few steps closer to his bride, as the doctor had suggested for this test, and then repeated, "What's for dinner?"

Still no response. Then he moved directly behind her and shouted, "What's for dinner?"

His wife spun around and loudly exclaimed, "For the third time—pot roast! What are you, deaf!?!"

"Are you hurt bad?"
"Ever heard of anyone hurt good?"

Doctors wear masks because of their fees!

Patient: Doctor, thank you for making my memory come back.
Doctor: Forget it!

At college I took medicine for four years. I wasn't cured, but I kept on taking it.

Patient: I've got a ringing in my ears.
Doctor: Don't answer it.

He has a pacemaker. Every time he burps, a garage door opens.

They're sealing medicine so tightly now, sick people can't get to it.

He's a doctor who treats only hypochondriacs. Of course, he only thinks he's a doctor.

Doctor: You owe me $10 for my advice.
Patient: Here's $2. My advice is to take it.

There's a guy that's flat on his back in the hospital. He got run over by a steamroller. He's in room 125 through 129.

My proctologist used to be a photographer. He told me to bend over and say cheese.

Patient: I feel like a deck of cards.
Doctor: I'll deal with you later.

He was in such pain. He kept calling for Elvis Presley's doctor.

Dad was always very good at fixing things, but he still had the occasional mishap. Once, he was fixing something using super glue and accidently glued his fingers together on one hand. It took a doctor and some patience to get them unstuck.

—Michelle, Wayne's daughter

My doctor told me I had six months to live. I didn't pay the bill. He gave me six more months.

Perfect cure for insomnia. Get plenty of sleep.

Patient: Doctor, I have an awful pain every time I lift my arm.

Doctor: So, don't lift it.

He's an M.D.—Mentally Deficient.

He's just as smart as he can be . . . unfortunately.

Never go to a doctor whose house plants have died.

Never agree to plastic surgery if the doctor's office is full of paintings by Picasso.

My short-term memory is not as sharp as it used to be. Also, my short-term memory is not as sharp as it used to be.

"Doc, I swallowed a bullet."
"Point yourself the other way."

I have kleptomania, but when it gets bad I take something for it.

8

Education and School

I started kindergarten on my fifth birthday: August 28, 1956. I apparently screamed my head off when my mother left me with my teacher.

In the second grade, I wet my pants. Miss McGavick said I had to wait five more minutes before I could go. I tried, but while I was painting at the easel I lost all control. To add insult to injury, the cutest girl in the school, Trudy Lithgoe, came up to talk to me, saw the puddle I was standing in, and started to laugh. That sent the entire class into an uproar. And little Wayne Osmond just stood there by the easel, brush in hand, red as a beet. Despite these early life-defining experiences (that I should probably still work out in therapy), I had such a passion for learning that I loved to go to school.

As a child, I especially loved books. I would get ahold of every book I could and read late into the night when everyone else was asleep. I wanted to know how things worked, so I read about them in the encyclopedia. I wondered how leaves and trees were structured, so I read about them in the encyclopedia. My brothers dubbed me the nerd of the family, because I wanted to read in my free time.

I was so interested in learning, I needed a place of my own to study and think.

In our house in California, we had one large room where all seven boys slept in bunk beds. We had a great time, but it was difficult to read and study in there—Alan and Merrill always had some kind of ball game or entrepreneurial endeavor going on. One day, I told my mother that I needed my own space to study. It was a significant request: our home was small and there were a lot of people in the family. But my mother, knowing how much I loved to learn, came through for me. She dubbed the tiny extra bathroom "Wayne's study" and brought in a desk.

Olive Osmond

We noticed early what a great memory Wayne had. He would memorize words to a song almost immediately, and it was unbelievable how he could recall names, places and dates.

When we started the correspondence courses he seemed to like math quite well, so he took first a basic math course. Then business math, algebra, geometry, trigonometry and slide rule. He got A's in all of his lessons and did them without the help of a teacher.

He would lock himself in a tiny little room by the music room in Arleta and concentrate for hours at a time until he got the answers.

As Marie once described to my daughter Amy, "The bathroom was so small, there wasn't even room for a chair. Wayne sat his little bottom on the toilet and studied at the desk in front of him for hours on end."

I often apologize to my posterity for passing on my pointed ears and susceptibility to athlete's foot; but it appears I have passed on a positive quality, as well. One day, my daughter Amy couldn't find her son Jacob, anywhere. He had been missing for at least half an hour, so she started calling for him—with no answer. Finally, she noticed that the upstairs bathroom door was locked. "Jake," she called. "Are you in the bathroom?"

"Yes," he replied.

"Are you okay? You've been in there for a long time."

"I'm fine," he said. "Just reading."

I'm thinking of buying him a desk to put in there.

Jokes

Why does *cleave* mean both "split apart" and "stick together?"

Why is "phonics" not spelled the way it sounds?

Why is "abbreviation" such a long word?

What's another word for "thesaurus?"

Is there another word for "synonym?"

Quoting one is plagiarism. Quoting many is research.

Why isn't the number 11 pronounced "onety-one?"

Who yelled, "Coming are the British?" Paul Reverse.

I'm reading this book about anti-gravity. Can't put it down!

I'm writing a book. I've got the page numbers done.

He recently finished his last book. At least people hope it is his last!

This book is selling like wildfire. That's because everyone is burning them.

"Joey, you have your shoes on the wrong feet."
"Teach, these are the only feet I have!"

The teacher asked, "How many make a million?"
Little Pete answered, "Not many!"

"Son, I'm worried about your being at the bottom of the class."
"Pop, they teach the same stuff at both ends!"

"How many wars has the USA fought in its history?"
"Eight."
"Name them."
"One, two, three, four, five, six, seven, eight!"

For every student with a spark of brilliance, there are about ten with ignition trouble.

I went to parachute-jumping class. The dropout rate was incredible!

She's one of those unemployed school teachers—no class and no principles!

A teacher asked, "What did Paul Revere say at the end of his famous ride?"
A student answered, "Whoa!"

I've been learning speed reading. Yesterday I read the complete works of Dickens. But then I had nothing to do for the rest of the evening.

Some kids want to know why the teachers get paid when it's the kids who have to do all the work.

The teacher asked, "How many of you children want to go to heaven?" All but one boy raised their hands. He said, "I can't. I have to go home right after school."

I once played hooky from school. My teacher sent my parents a thank-you note!

Don't use a big word where a diminutive one will suffice.

Don't let school interfere with your education.

F u cn rd ths u cnt spl wrth a drn!

Fairy tales are horror stories for children to get them used to reality.

From sharp minds come . . . pointed heads.

Minds are like parachutes . . . they only work when they're open.

Proofread carefully to see if you any words out.

Teachers have class.

Did you hear about the cannibal who was expelled from school? He was buttering up his teacher.

What do the letters D.N.A. stand for? National Dyslexics Association.

What does an envelope say when you lick it? Nothing, it just shuts up.

Why was six afraid of seven? Because seven eight nine!

I'm trying to write with this broken pencil but it's pointless.

I've written several children's books. I didn't mean to—they just turned out that way.

My grade point average was so low, the dean appointed a football player to tutor me.

Many people have not heard about my alma mater. Let me assure you, It's one of the goodest in the United States.

He's majoring in communications and minoring in philosophy. Now he can wonder out loud.

I'm educated beyond my intelligence.

Whose cruel idea was it to put an "S" in the word *lisp* and to put three "T's" in the word *stutter?*

Why is the alphabet in that order? Is it because of that song?

"Mom, why am I the tallest kid in the third grade? Is it because I'm Welch?"
"No, it's because you're eighteen."

I won't say what kind of student he was, but the teacher would give him extra credit for being absent.

One time Donny, Marie, and I had an opportunity to ride with the Blue Angels. I was a flight instructor at the time so the pilot I went up with teasingly said that he was going to make me really sick. Once we were up in the air, he asked me if I wanted to fly the plane. Of course I was just hoping I'd get the chance, so I kept spinning and spinning the plane because it was so fun. This A-4 airplane could spin 360 degrees twice in one second. Wow! What a great time I had! After landing, I noticed that the pilot looked a little sick.

—*Wayne*

Sam had just completed his first day at school. "What did you learn today?" asked his mother. "Not enough," said Sam. "I have to go back tomorrow."

Suzie: Mother, I can't go to school today.
Mother: Why not?
Suzie: I don't feel well.
Mother: Where don't you feel well?
Suzie: In school.

He was a fast learner and a quick forgetter.

It was a raw, rainy day in upstate New York; but Mom, as usual, was bright and cheerful. As she went to wake up her son, he protested, "No, Ma, I don't want to go to school."
"Buy why not, son? Give me two good reasons why you don't want to get up."
"Well, for one, the kids hate me and, for another, the teachers hate me, too."
"Oh, that's no reason not to go to school. Come on now—get ready."
"Give me two good reasons why I should go to school," the son demanded.
"Well, for one, you're 46 years old. And for another, you're the principal."

Grandma: And how do you like going to school, Billy?
Billy: I like going, and I like coming back. It's the part in between I don't like.

Father: What's the meaning of those "D's" and "F's" on your report card?
Son: Oh, Dad, that means I'm doing fine.

I got an "A" in philosophy because I proved that my professor didn't exist.

Horace: Day after day the boy and his dog went to
          school together until at last the day came
          when they had to part.
Morris: What happened?
Horace: The dog graduated.

Jonathon had trouble pronouncing the letter "R," so his teacher gave him this sentence to practice at home: "Robert gave Richard a rap in the rib for roasting the rabbit so rare." Some days later the teacher asked him to say the sentence to her. Jonathon rattled it off: "Bob gave Dick a poke in the side for not cooking the bunny enough."

He got A's in high school: "Ay sit down! Ay shut up!"

9

Famous and Not-So-Famous People

I have had a great time meeting a wide variety of people throughout the years; and having been in show business for more than half a century, I've met a lot of people. Some of my kids' favorite stories are about the famous people I've met. When they were young, they loved to watch "Entertainment Tonight" with me and ask, "Have you met that person?" whenever someone was featured. They loved hearing about the time that we were invited to Elvis Presley's house and ended up giving him a Book of Mormon, which he promised to read. They thought it was hilarious when we told them about Merrill licking his lips in front of the Queen of England and later being "busted" in the tabloids for sticking out his tongue at the Queen. They were especially interested in the friendly rivalry between the Osmonds and the Jackson Five in the 1970s and thought it was so cool when Michael Jackson would come over to Donny's or Jimmy's house.

When we were young, my brothers and I were in a TV special with Kurt Russell opening up the Haunted Mansion Ride at Disneyland. We rode through that ride at least a hundred times so they could get just the right angles, the right dialogue, and the right expressions on film. By that time, we knew the ride forwards and backwards. We knew where all of the triggers for the animatronics were and would go activate them, trying to scare each other. We figured out how all of the ghosts worked—which was a feat, because it was high-tech back then. We knew how to prompt the movies that would come on and would watch them over and over. Kurt and I were good friends throughout that special and when we worked together in the show, "The Travels of Jamie McPheeters."

While meeting famous people has always been invigorating, over the years I have become more interested

---

September 6, 1966

California

Today we slept in and then at 1:00 p.m we were at NBC. First we worked with Jonny Horton (one of the Good Time Singers) until 2:00 (which was our original call) and then worked with Mr. Wyle. Andy sang "Tumbling Tumble Weeds" with us, and then Merrill played the banjo for him. He said (jokingly), "You're going to end up as a lounge act." He's right, but we want a little versatility.

After, we worked with Johnny Horton for 2 hours and then went to R-3 and worked with our new choreographer (Jack Regas) and Maggie Banks on our cowboy routine. It's hard! We went home and I'll bet we went through it 30 times! We went to bed sweating and exhausted.

in spending time with people who are not as famous but perhaps more interesting.

Jokes

Did you hear about the cross-eyed teacher who couldn't control his pupils?

How do you spell that? Wrong every time.

Miss Jones had been giving her second-grade students a lesson on science. She had explained about magnets and showed how they would pick up nails and other bits of iron. Now it was question time, and she said, "My name begins with the letter 'M' and I pick up things. What am I?" A little boy on the front row said, "You're a mother."

A new teacher tries to make good use of her psychology courses. The first day of class, she starts by saying, "Everyone who thinks they're stupid, stand up." After a few seconds, Little Johnny stands up. The teacher asks, "Do you think you're stupid, Johnny?" "No, ma'am, but I hate to see you standing there all by yourself."

Did you hear that Willie Nelson got hit by a car? He was playing on the road again.

Do you know who Picabo Street is? Well, she just donated a bunch of money to build a new hospital wing. They are going to call it the Peek-a-Boo ICU.

Did you hear about Vanna White? She's in rehab—she's hooked on phonics.

You know who Mahatma Gandhi was? Well, he used to walk everywhere, which made his feet calloused. He didn't eat much, so he was weak and frail. People actually thought he was mystical. And what he did eat was very strange, which gave him very bad breath. He was known as the super calloused fragile mystic hexed by halitosis.

Why did Humpty Dumpty have a great fall? He wanted to make up for the lousy summer.

Why was Cinderella so lousy at baseball? She ran away from the ball, and she had a pumpkin for a coach.

(To a man named John) Oh, I've been to your room.

Once I had a psychic girlfriend. She left me before we met.

Do you know how to catch a unique person? You 'neak up on them.

What do you call four bullfighters in quicksand? Quattro sinko.

I called the Psychic Friends Network just for fun. They said, "Who's calling?" I said, "You tell me."

I went to the Miss America contest and everyone was there: Miss New York, Miss Georgia, Miss Utah, and Miss Cellaneous .

Why is the Miss Universe contest always won by someone from Earth?

He was bowlegged and she was knock-kneed. When they stood together, they spelled the word "ox!"

The cure for love at first sight is to take another look.

Do you know why Native Americans were the first people on this continent? They had reservations.

The Lone Ranger looked up at the hills to the west and said to Tonto, "There's a big war party of Sioux on the top of that hill."

Tonto said, "We will go to the east."
The Lone Ranger said, "There are Pawnees approaching from the east."
"We will go south, kemosabe."
"Osages."

Greg, Dad, and I once went to Bob Hope's house to film him for an anti-drug commercial. At the time, Dad was working on a project for a guy and had solicited Mr. Hope's help. My first clue that Dad was a little bit nervous to bring us along was that he made Greg and me get dressed up in our suits and ties—and Dad even combed our hair. Not a normal occurrence for him.

Our second clue that Dad was nervous to bring us into a professional setting was that on our way to Bob Hope's house, Dad drove the wrong way on a one-way street. As I looked out the window, all I could see was a mass of cars driving toward us. Dad laid on the horn and pulled a five-lane u-turn to flip it around, as Greg and I held on for dear life and dodged dishes falling out of the cupboards of our motorhome.

We checked into a Marriott in downtown L.A. so Dad could shave and wash his hair. Then we really knew that Dad wanted to make a good impression. He hates to shave.

Dad came out shortly, and away we went to Bob Hope's house. It was the most uneventful part of the trip. We were perfect angels, so Dad didn't have to worry. Bob Hope was a nice guy and just as funny in person.

—*Steve, Wayne's son*

"North?"

"It looks like a million Blackfeet in the north."

"Tonto, what if they attack us? What will we do?"

Tonto started to mount up, saying, "What do you mean 'we,' white man?"

A friend in need is a pest, indeed.

Bore: A person who has nothing to say and says it.

Boys will be boys, but one day all girls will be women.

Clones are people two.

Eli Whitney's last words: "Keep your hands off my cotton pickin' gin."

John Doe was a nobody.

"Luck" is my middle name . . . mind you, my first name is "Bad."

Mad at your neighbor? Buy his kid a drum!

The average man is proof enough that women can take a joke.

When confronted by a difficult problem, you can solve it more easily by reducing it to the question, "How would the Lone Ranger handle this?"

Did you hear about the guy who ran through the screen door? He strained himself.

How can you recognize a burned-out hippie? He used to take acid; now he takes antacid.

What do you call a rabbit with fleas? Bugs Bunny.

Why are cowboy hats turned up at the sides? So three cowboys can ride in a pickup truck.

I do the work of three men: Larry, Moe, and Curly.

He does the work of two men: Laurel and Hardy.

He's done for music what Jackie Gleason did for the sport of pole vaulting.

Why do cowboys need two spurs? Are they afraid one side of the horse might take off galloping by itself?

Why did Eve move to New York?
She fell for the Big Apple.

But when I was down there at Star Trek I found out some things. For instance, do you know why Captain Kirk hears so well? Because he's got a right ear, a left ear . . . and a final front ear.

He's a great family man, like Charles Manson.

As President, he was so boring that when he had fireside chats, the fire would go out.

Does the name Pavlov ring a bell?

Eve: Adam, do you love me?
Adam: Who else?

When blondes have more fun, do they know it?

Mary had a little lamb who liked to stand by the heater. and every time he wagged his tail, he burned his little seater.

10

Food, Dining, and Diets

I definitely have my favorite foods, just like anybody else. The difference is that when I find a food I like, I eat that food—pretty much exclusively. In the mid-nineties, my pick was shortbread cookies. It was the only food I could keep down after my brain surgery. In the late nineties, I was into Twinkies and Ding Dongs for a while. During the 2000's, water popcicles, fudge bars, pistachios, and carrots were my main sources of nutrition. In 2008, I was partial to 40-calorie hot dogs, but that proved to be only a transitional phase, as I soon after discovered beef jerky.

Following years of experimentation, I've come up with my own weight-loss diet plan, which you will find exclusively in this book. It's free, plus the cost of food. The secret is this: eat raw carrots without peeling for extra minerals. I eat 6 to 8 every day, all day, but you can eat as many as you would like. Add a side of sliced meat, beef nuggets, or jerky. You will lose a pound a day, guaranteed.

My doctor would definitely not recommend this diet plan, however. Following a year of heavy carrot eating, he diagnosed me with Carotenoderma, which basically means that my skin had turned orange. Kathy told me to lay off the carrots; Merrill, Jay, and Jimmy told me I looked like I had bathed in sunless tanning lotion. But I liked it because it made me look tan on stage. So I'd say, "I like being orange—it's my favorite color." And the carrot eating continued. Sounds far-fetched, I know. My family would be the first to tell you that it's pretty accurate. But not healthy.

When I do stray from my one-item diets, I have a few staple menu items that I like to prepare. Now, I'm no chef, but I think these recipes are pretty good. My kids wanted me to include my concoctions, but I'm not sure whether it's because they like my food or because they *don't* like my food. You be the judge.

Wonky's Nutritious Juice

4 or 5 carrots

1 large red beet

2 Granny Smith apples

2 stalks celery

2 tomatoes

brewer's yeast

Wash vegetables and fruit, then cut into pieces to fit into juicer.

I started making this juice twenty years ago when my kids were still little. Because my eating habits are a little unorthodox, I need to make this juice somewhat frequently so I get all of my vitamins. This juice is very nutritious and actually tastes pretty good. One caution: it stains.

Wonk's On-the-Road Lemonade

1 lemon (Slices can usually be found next to the fountain drinks at most restaurants. Just use enough to equal 1 lemon.)

8 individual packets of sugar

Simply squeeze all the juice from one lemon into a tall glass of water. Add 8 packets of sugar. Stir, and *voila!* A nice cool drink, but not heavy like lemonade.

This is my favorite makeshift drink. It tastes good and is a great icebreaker for dinner parties. Once they see you at work, they have a lot to talk about.

Wonk the Donk Sandwich

1 slice white bread

Worcestershire sauce

4 or 5 slices of provolone cheese

Pour plenty of Worcestershire sauce on a slice of white bread. Top with several slices of provolone cheese. Microwave until the edges of the cheese start to bubble. You've got yourself a Wonk the Donk Sandwich!

I once made this sandwich for a man named Bob. He loved it! Of course, he was my tile man, and I hadn't paid him for his services, yet. He also enjoyed the Lean Cuisine I made for him.

Pistachio Cuisine

1 32-ounce bag of pistachio nuts without the shells

Stuff as many as you can into your mouth at one time, remembering that your cheeks can also be utilized for storage area. Enjoy! I do this all the time. They last at least 20 minutes if you savor them.

Yes, it's usually better to indulge in this recipe when you're alone. Or when you're really comfortable with someone.

White Bread, Peanut Butter, Banana, Pickle, and Smoked Turkey Sandwich

Always use white bread. Put plenty of creamy peanut butter on a slice of bread (at least ½ inch thick). Place thinly sliced bananas on the peanut butter. Top with bread and butter pickles (as many as you want, but at least three). Add at least ½ of an inch of thinly sliced smoked turkey. Cover the top with another slice of bread, and man! That's a sandwich!

There's not a lot of mystery to this sandwich. You use white bread, peanut butter, bananas, pickles, and smoked turkey, just as the name suggests. The trick is in the order and quantity of the ingredients.

Easy Cheesy Sandwich

Easy Cheese, you pick the flavor

1 piece of bread

Unload ½ of the can of Easy Cheese onto one piece of bread.

My granddaughter, Maia, is especially fond of this sandwich. She loves it so much, she asked her mom to make it every day of kindergarten. Guess what her mom said.

Dad's Beans

6 cans vegetarian baked beans

3 cans spicy stewed tomatoes

Take the cans of beans and empty them into a large pan. Add the cans of spicy stewed tomatoes. Simmer. Stir about every 15 minutes for a few hours.

Surprisingly, this is the only meal that my family has ever asked me to make for them. It takes a few hours to really combine the flavors, so make these when you have some time on your hands. And never mix these beans with onions. It makes tear gas!

Jokes

A balanced diet is a cookie in each hand.

I have a question. Can vegetarians eat animal crackers?

What do you call cheese that doesn't belong to you? Nacho Cheese

If carrots are so good for the eyes, how come I see so many dead rabbits on the highway?

Health nuts are going to feel stupid someday, lying in hospitals, dying of nothing.

If a parsley farmer goes bankrupt, do they garnish his wages?

If corn oil comes from corn, where does baby oil come from?

If you ate pasta and antipasta, would you still be hungry?

Did you hear about the restaurant on the moon? The food is terrific, but there's no atmosphere.

Why is there an expiration date on sour cream?

Never, never, cook onions and beans together! It makes tear gas!

Do you know what kind of coffee they served on the Titanic? Sanka!

Dad and I have a few things in common. We are both left-handed. We have both left our groceries at the store (for hours) after paying for them. We both enjoy a tall glass of Mountain Dew and tell everyone we're drinking it for medicinal purposes. And we both love eating banana splits.

A few years ago, Dad started a tradition. On his birthday, Dad takes anyone who is in town to Baskin Robbins for a large banana split. I always try to make sure I'm in town for that celebration.

—Amy, Wayne's daughter

Do you know what you get when you throw a grenade into a French kitchen? Linoleum blownapart.

A guy goes into a library and says to the librarian, "I'll have a hamburger, shake and fries!" She says, "Sir, this is a library!" "OK," he whispers. "I'll have a hamburger, shake, and fries."

Why don't cannibals eat clowns? They taste funny.

A clean tie will always attract the soup of the day.

Getting into hot water keeps you clean.

Bagels have been around for centuries—the ones I bought yesterday even longer!

A cannibal is a man who loves his fellow men . . . with gravy.

A cannibal is a guy who goes into a restaurant and orders a waiter.

The doctor told me to think thin. I did and lost four inches around my head.

I went on a no-starch diet. But I can eat all the bleach and detergent I want.

I can't believe it happened. The other day I jogged backwards and put on eight pounds!

It's hard for a five-foot-six father to explain to his six-foot-one son why junk food is bad for you!

A woman spent months trying to poison her husband. She didn't know that he was immune because he ate in the company cafeteria!

I adore seafood, especially saltwater taffy!

I once had a meal in a German-Chinese restaurant. The food was delicious, but an hour later I was hungry for power!

I've been drinking lots of carrot juice because it's good for my eyes. But I'm wondering if I'm overdoing it. When I try to sleep, I can see through my eyelids!

I have to spend a lot of money on food. My family won't eat anything else.

Our family moved to Bountiful, Utah, when I was in eighth grade. Every weekend, someone would have a party, so I decided to take a turn. Mom sent Dad down to get some refreshments for my party. Dad practically bought out the junk food aisle. We had Twinkies, Ding Dongs, Ho-Ho's, chips, candy, pop—at least ten times the amount of food that I had seen at any other party. Dad was at the top of everyone's "favorite dad list" after that.

—*Greg, Wayne's son*

I went to a salad bar in Detroit. They change the oil every six months!

"I'm so hungry I could eat a horse."
"You've come to the right place!"

I watch my weight. I have it right out in front of me where I can see it!

Eat yogurt and get culture.

Every time I lose weight, it finds me again.

Lose weight—put a scale in front of the fridge.

No matter how you slice it, it's still baloney.

Plastic packaged foods are very uncanny.

Prunes give you a run for your money.

What's the difference between boogers and broccoli? Kids won't eat broccoli.

Never attempt to put on a pullover sweater while eating a caramel apple.

Raisins are important. Without them thousands of gingerbread men wouldn't be able to see.

What does cheese say when it gets its picture taken?

(At restaurant) What's today's special, the Heimlich maneuver?

I'm not working out. My philosophy? No pain, no pain.

On a diet? Go to the paint store. You can get thinner there.

Did you hear the joke about the sandwich? Never mind. It's a lot of baloney.

Johnny: (offering some candy) Here, Janey,
           sweets to the sweet!
Janey: Oh, thank you; and won't you have some
           of these nuts?

Lose weight—eat stuff you hate.

What kind of shoes are made from banana skins?
Slippers.

I have to exercise in the morning before my brain figures
out what I'm doing.

The advantage of exercising every day is that you die
healthier.

A snail bought a particularly impressive racecar and decided to enter the Indianapolis 500. To give the car a
distinctive look, the snail had a big letter "S" painted on
the hood, sides, and trunk before the big race. When the
race began, the snail's car immediately took the lead,
prompting one of the spectators to say, "Look at that 'S'
car go!"

Customer: Waiter, why does this doughnut look all
           crushed?
Waiter: Well, you said, "coffee and a doughnut,
           and step on it."

I sure gained a lot of weight during the holidays last year.
It was ridiculous. In January I went to a zoo, and the elephants were throwing peanuts at me!

The second day of a diet is always easier than the first.
By the second day you're off it.

What do you call a doll that's on fire? A Barbie-Q.

(To a dove) Don't worry, I'm a vegetarian.

Food is so expensive, it is cheaper to eat money.

M&M's melt in your mouth, not in your hand. But what do they do under your arm?

Waiter: I hope the chili wasn't too spicy.
Customer: No, I always bleed from the ears.

The cook is so bad, he burns salad.

The steak is so bad, it still has marks where the jockey hit it.

These hors d'oeuvres melt in your mouth. They're ice cubes.

Customer: Why is your thumb on my steak?
Waiter: I don't wanna drop it again.

She makes food fit for a king. Here, King!

No one cooks like she does. The Army came close.

She is such a bad cook that I bought her an oven that flushes.

One time, Dad picked up some burritos for us between shows from a fast-food joint. After eating my delicious burrito, I came across some hard things on my last bite. After spitting them out, I realized that I had almost swallowed three fingernail clippings. Dad was so upset that he immediately drove over to the establishment and talked to the manager. He didn't stop there. I heard him call and talk directly to an executive of the corporation.

—*Greg, Wayne's son*

She used popcorn in the pancakes so they turned over by themselves.

She's so fat that when mosquitoes see her, they scream, "Buffet!"

(While eating) This isn't half bad—it's all bad.

I went on a raw fish diet. I didn't lose any weight, but you should see me swim.

I just got off a ten day diet. I lost a week and a half.

I'm trying to get back to my original weight: 8 pounds, 8 ounces.

You know that it's time to diet when the doctor tells you that the mysterious rash on your stomach is a steering-wheel burn.

Warden: What would you like for your last meal?
Prisoner: Something to go.

Never forget that stressed spelled backwards is "desserts."

I'm not saying she's a bad cook, but I don't think meatloaf should glow in the dark.

The four food groups: fast, frozen, instant, and chocolate.

Eat well, stay fit, die anyway.

"I thought you were trying to get into shape?"
"I am. The shape I've selected is a triangle."

Thou shalt not weigh more than thy refrigerator.

Beans are the reason most of Mexico is located out-of-doors.

11

Old Age

One day I needed to run an errand. I jumped in the car and drove all the way down the street, turned the corner and drove a little farther, turned left, and went down a main street for about 2 miles until I was next to the freeway. I stopped because I couldn't remember why I had driven down there, so I drove all the way back up to the house. I went in the house and still couldn't remember what I was going to do. I did notice I had left my wallet on the kitchen counter, so I picked it up and drove down the street again. I drove down by the freeway again and still couldn't remember what I was supposed to do, so I parked in the parking lot at Walgreens for about 20 minutes until I finally remembered what the errand was. I remember going up and down the street that day but don't recall what for now. Unfortunately, that's a true story.

Old age jokes are always crowd pleasers. Young people like them, because it reminds them of how young they are. Middle-aged people like them, because it reminds them that they still have a lot of mileage left. And old people like them, because by that time they've learned not to take life too seriously, anyway.

Jokes

Middle age is when broadness of the mind and narrowness of the waist change places.

Be nice to your kids. They'll choose your nursing home.

The older you get, the tougher it is to lose weight, because by then your body and your fat are really good friends.

Wrinkled was not one of the things I wanted to be when I grew up.

"Your tights are all wrinkled."
"But I'm not wearing any!"

A con man was selling a magic elixir guaranteed to make people live forever. "Take a good look at me," the con man said to the crowd of older people gathered outside the supermarket. "Feast your eyes on a man who is two hundred and fifty years old."

An old man asked the con man's young assistant, "Is he really that old?"

The assistant said, "I don't know. I've only been working for him for seventy-five years!"

You know you're old if you can remember when bacon, eggs, and sunshine were good for you.

You know, there are three things that happen when you get old. The first one is you lose your memory, and I can't remember the other two.

You know you're getting old when the candles cost more than the cake.

I'm really glad to be here. At my age I'm glad to be anywhere.

Folks, I am so old I remember when the Dead Sea was only sick.

A guy came up to me the other day and said, "Do you wear boxers or briefs?" I said, "Well, Depends."

I'm so old I remember when fast food was an antelope.

A guy came up to me the other day and complimented me on my alligator shoes. I was walking barefoot.

I said to my sweetheart, "Honey, will you still love me when I am old and feeble?" She said, "Of course, I do."

An old man is sitting on a park bench, sobbing, and a young man walks by and asks him what's wrong. The old man says, "I'm married to a beautiful twenty-two-year-old woman." The young man says, "What's wrong with that?" And the old man says, "I forgot where I live!"

He can't go out with girls his own age because there aren't any!

If you think things improve with the years, attend a class reunion.

You know you're getting on in years when the commercial for hair restorer is more interesting than the show.

They're having an age problem. He won't act his, and she won't tell hers.

A man of indeterminate age checked with a doctor to see if the doctor could tell him how old he was. After a quick examination, the doctor said, "According to the examination, I'm alone in this room!"

An older man states his intention to marry a girl of twenty. A friend says, "Such a marriage could be fatal." The man answers, "So she'll die!"

Everything's just starting to click for me—my elbows, my neck, my knees!

Doctor: You should live to be eighty.
Patient: I'm eighty-five.
Doctor: See—what did I tell you!

For someone up in years, weightlifting consists of standing up!

"Grandpa, why don't you get a hearing aid?"
"Don't need it. I hear more than I can understand!"

If you don't wear your specs when you look in the mirror, you'll eliminate wrinkles!

"To what do you attribute your old age?"
"I was born a long time ago!"

Mr. Foster wanted a transplant. The hospital explained that they no longer made the parts!

He's so old, when he lit the candles on his cake, it started the smoke alarm.

You've reached middle age when all you exercise is caution.

He is so old, he flew before the skies were friendly.

He worked his head to the bone.

One ninety-year-old man married a woman of the same age. Spent their honeymoon trying to get out of the car!

He knew he'd be bald. People said that he'd come out on top.

Science has found that there is only one thing to prevent baldness—hair!

I'm so old I remember when sushi was called bait.

A child asks his mother, "What did Daddy look like a long time ago?" The mother answers, "He had long dark hair with natural waves." The kid said, "Well, who's the old baldheaded coot who lives with us now?"

A baldheaded man asks a druggist for some hair restorer. The druggist offers him a very expensive concoction, but he wants to know if it really works. The druggist says, "Does it work? I accidentally spilled some on my comb, and now it's a brush!"

His hair was as white as snow, but somebody shoveled it off!

He once had very wavy hair. Now he's only got beach left.

One woman nagged her bald husband so much his scalp turned gray.

The advantage of having a toupee is that you can go see a movie while your hair is being shampooed!

Getting old has its advantages. Your friends can come to your birthday party and warm themselves around your cake.

"It's my birthday."
"Many happy returns. How old aren't you?"

She's like an old shoe. Everything's worn out but the tongue.

She must be older than she says she is. She has a recipe for curds and whey!

Old age—when you turn from stud to dud!

She sighed, "You used to kiss me." He kissed her.
"You used to hold my hand." He held her hand.

"You used to bite me on the back of my neck."
"Hold on."
"Where are you going?"
"To get my teeth!"

A widow was fixed up on a blind date with a ninety-year-old man. When she returned home later, her daughter asked, "How did it go?" The widow said, "I had to slap his face three times." "He got fresh?" "No, I thought he was dead!"

Wrinkles are hereditary. Mothers and fathers get them from the kids.

The best way to keep looking young is to hang out with old people!

Age isn't important unless you're a cheese.

By the time a man finds greener pastures, he's too old to climb the fence.

Cosmetics: A woman's means for keeping a man from reading between the lines.

Few women admit their age. Few men act theirs.

Going the speed of light is bad for your age.

Gravity brings you down.

Seen it all, done it all, can't remember most of it.

The biggest thing wrong with the younger generation is that a lot of us don't belong to it, anymore.

The market for toupees is thinning.

The only advantage of old age is that you can sing while you brush your teeth.

I'm so old my knees will buckle, but my belt won't.

Why did the man put wheels on his rocking chair? He wanted to rock and roll.

An old person sent me a postcard. It said, "Wish you were here. Where am I?"

Age is contagious. You get it from birthday candles.

I'm so old, I knew the first of the Mohicans.

I'm so old, when people say, "Remember the Alamo," I do.

I'm so old, I don't buy green bananas anymore.

I'm so old, every morning I hear snap, crackle, pop, and it's not coming from my cereal.

I'm so old, everything I want for Christmas can be purchased at a drugstore.

Did you hear about the lady with the "Gleem" in her eye? Her toothbrush slipped.

I'm so old, my doctor told me to slow down; so I got a job with the post office.

My doctor said I look like a million bucks—green and wrinkled.

I'm so old, I walked past a cemetery and two boys ran after me with shovels.

Do you know the formula for a long life? Keep breathing.

You know you are getting old when you and your teeth don't sleep together.

You know you are getting old when your address book has mostly names that start with Dr.

He was born the year they invented rope.

You know you are getting old when you sit in a rocking chair and can't get it going.

You know you are getting old when it takes twice as long to look half as good.

You know you are getting old when everything hurts, and what doesn't hurt doesn't work.

Be true to your teeth and they won't be false to you.

It's no longer a question of staying healthy. It's a question of finding a sickness that you like.

When the home for the aged came to him for a donation, he gave them his mother and father.

He keeps his wife's teeth with him so she can't eat between meals.

Today is the 10th anniversary of her 29th birthday.

Fifty years old isn't old. If you were a turtle, you'd be a baby.

He's at the age now that when he sinks his teeth into a steak, they stay there.

He is in the prime of his senility.

Every night, like the stars, her teeth come out.

You know you're getting old when you stoop to tie your shoes and wonder what else you can do while you're down there.

Quit worrying about your health—it'll go away.

Life begins at forty, if you're getting out of prison.

12

Hobbies

My first memory was the summer of 1954, when I was just about to turn three years old. I was sitting on my father's shoulders at the Ogden Airport, watching the USAF Thunderbirds flying the F-100 Super Sabers. They were loud and fast. I thought, "Boy! That's for me!"

From that time on, all I could think about was airplanes, airplanes, and airplanes. I would take a notebook with me all the time and draw all sorts of different kinds of machines with wings on them. In fact, later on in life my nickname became "Wings." I started learning all the names of the different military fighter jets and transport planes. I learned all the civilian planes' names. I made at least 80 different model airplanes and hung them all from the ceiling over my bunk bed. I just couldn't get enough of these beautiful machines that defied gravity.

When I found out that the government provided free books about airplanes on how they worked and all the information necessary to actually pass your written exam for a pilot's license, I was in seventh heaven! I sent away for all the free books I could get.

First, I just studied about the different makes and models of airplanes and what keeps an airplane in the air.

As I grew older, I delved more into the technicalities of flying, such as plotting, omnigation, ADF (aerial direction finding), DME (distance measuring equipment), ATC (air traffic control) transponders, instrument flying, and radio communication. Then, when I was sixteen, one of our family friends (a pilot) found out that I was interested in flying and arranged a flying lesson for me.

My father and I went to the airport, I met my instructor, and we proceeded to the airplane—a 172 Cessna. After making a preflight check of the airplane and its cockpit, we started up the engine, received Ground Control clearance, taxied into position, made our final engine run-up check, received Tower Clearance, and then lowered our flaps slightly before racing down the runway for our take-off. When we reached 80 mph, I eased back on the control wheel, and we were airborne. After reaching 5000 feet, we leveled off, trimmed the aircraft out, and began a series of maneuvers such as lazy eights, chandels, 720-degree turns, eights on and around pylons, stalls, and recoveries.

After about an hour of real excitement, we tuned into the Van Nuys Airport tower and received landing instructions. After the final approach, I cut the throttle. But when we were about ten feet off the ground, I applied too much back pressure on the control wheel and stalled the airplane, touching down three times before actually landing. That's called, "three for the price of one." Luckily, the instructor didn't give up on me and I got my pilot's license at age 17—two years before my driver's license. Since that time, I've received my private pilot's license, instrument rating, commercial license, flight instructor's certificate, and multi-engine license.

Donny and I were the two brothers that really liked airplanes, so one day I decided to give him the ride of a lifetime in my new Skylane. I did everything I could think of to scare him: tight turns, extreme wing waggles, and steep ascents and descents. But Donny just laughed the whole time.

My flying had to come to an end when I discovered I had cancer (there are strict rules surrounding operating a plane with a medical condition). But though I haven't been able to pilot a plane for years, I was recently able to be the copilot when Donny took Kathy and me up in his new airplane, an Aero Commander turboprop that he had bought to fly between Las Vegas and Utah. Donny had consulted with me about which airplane he should buy, so I was really excited for his plane to arrive.

March 18, 1965

Dear Diary:

Today I got up and got ready to take my first flying lesson. When we got there Jim London was waiting for me. He talked to a pilot teacher to get me a lesson free. Well we started off. I got to start the engine and the dials. We taxied on the runway. I called tower and said, "Van Nuys 76 Tango ready for take-off. We started on the runway. Soon as we hit 80 mph. I eased back on the wheel. As soon as we were at 5,000 feet I leveled off. I had to use the trim tab and that's a very touchy process. We went through turns, banks, glides, straight and level (trim tab) and climbs. He turned the engine down to idle and we glided and then he let me do it. I made a pretty bad landing but he said it wasn't so bad. We taxied over by the tower and I said, "Van Nuys tower 76 tango taxi to skyways." After that he signed my log book and then we went home.

The day after the plane was delivered, he invited me to take a trip with him, and he let me pick the place. I wanted to see Afton, Wyoming, which was settled by my great grandfather, George Osmond. I was so excited the night before to ride in Donny's new airplane that I couldn't even sleep.

On April 7, 2009, Donny, Debbie, and their son Donald (along with the pilot and another friend) picked Kathy and me up at the little airport near our home. From there, we flew to Afton, Wyoming. The day was sunny, brisk, and beautiful. We drove around the community, visited the cemetery where Great-Grandpa was buried, had some hot chocolate and a little lunch, and drove a little further to Osmond, Wyoming. I loved the whole trip; but of course my favorite part was sitting next to the pilot in the right seat and then taking my turn at the controls. Though I had set out to give Donny a great plane ride those many years ago, Donny was the one who gave me the ride of a lifetime!

Jokes

If at first you don't succeed, skydiving is definitely not for you!

The best place to be during an earthquake is bungee jumping.

Hey, you know what folks? Boomerangs are coming back.

What do you call a boomerang that doesn't work? A stick.

It's a good thing we have gravity, or else when birds die they would stay up there.

There's a fine line between fishing and standing on the shore looking like an idiot.

Never play leapfrog with a unicorn.

I'm a born hunter. Last week I went after ducks, and the decoy got away!

What has a hundred legs and lives on yogurt? An aerobic class!

A man lay spread out over three seats in the second row of a movie theater. As he lay there breathing heavily, an usher came over and said, "That's very rude of you, sir, taking up three seats. Didn't you learn any manners? Where did you come from?" The man looked up helplessly and said, "The balcony!"

The only game that can't be fixed is peek-a-boo.

We have a dozen bingo halls in our town. All the proceeds go to fight gambling.

When the chips are down, the buffalo is empty.

What do you call a frightened scuba diver? Chicken of the sea.

I've taken up meditation. At least that's better than sitting around doing nothing.

"This jigsaw puzzle is driving me crazy," said Hubert to his friend on the phone. "What's so difficult about it?" asked his buddy. "Well, for one, there are just so many pieces. They're all the same color and the edges aren't flat. They're crinkly." "What's the picture on the box?" his buddy inquired. "A big rooster," Hubert replied. "Okay Hubie, now listen very carefully. Pick up all the pieces and put the cornflakes back in the box."

I like dancing; and I like what you're doing, too.

The yo-yo was named after its inventor.

Old fisherman never die. They just smell that way.

Do you know what the difference is between a good pilot and a bad pilot? Well, a good pilot breaks ground and flies into the wind.

Today I got up and realized that this is my first birthday in quite a while that I'd be home. Everybody sang "Happy Birthday" and then I got a real nice book called "Who am I" and a 10 dollar bill to buy myself a three-in-one [triple combination of scriptures]!

We went to church (I was an usher) and after Sunday School we went home. Grandma Osmond and Verne were there and then we all went over home and ate a real good meal. I had three cakes! Alan and Virl took some pictures of me with my book and camera. (I got my camera in Sweden but it's my birthday present.)

Later Uncle Ralph and Aunt Lidya came up, left, and then Uncle Rulon, Aunt Norma and Darlene came up and went to Sacrament meeting with us. We went home and had some cake 'n' ice cream. Uncle Rulon's family left and then Grandma Osmond and Vern left and we went to bed.

13

Holidays

When Kathy and I had young children, we usually ate Christmas dinner with Kathy's family, then headed over to my Mother and Father's house for dessert and a relaxing evening. It wasn't always relaxing, but it was always fun! Marie and I would tell our favorite jokes, while Kathy and Jay would talk about the new books they were reading. I felt sorry for Donny—my kids and their cousins would chase him around the house. He is so ticklish, he was sincerely scared of them and would bolt down the halls to get away, much to my children's delight. Alan usually had his boys perform a song they were singing together, which was always a treat. And Merrill would make everyone feel great with his charistmatic personality and funny stories. In earlier days, Donny, Marie, and Jimmy would put on puppet shows for their nephews and nieces on Christmas Eve. Santa always seemed to have time to stop in on Christmas Eve, too.

One Christmas, Jimmy gave every individual family a big toy electric train that we'd set up to go around the Christmas tree. We still keep the tradition and set up the train for our grandchildren and children to enjoy.

I am especially excited at Christmas to spend time with Virl and Tom. Virl and I spent a lot of time together as young kids. He was the oldest and used to take care of me when Mother needed an extra hand. Because of this, we have a strong, lifetime bond. As our families and businesses took off in different directions, we didn't always get to see each other as much as we would have liked. But I knew I would always get to see him at Christmas, and that made my visits to Mother and Father's especially gratifying. It was the same with Tom. He has lived in Ephraim, Utah, for many years, which was several hours away from my parents' house in Provo and a long

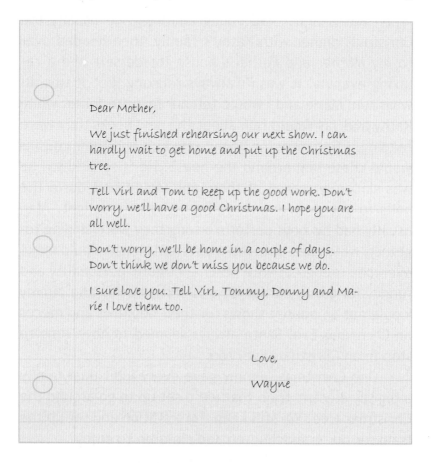

Dear Mother,

We just finished rehearsing our next show. I can hardly wait to get home and put up the Christmas tree.

Tell Virl and Tom to keep up the good work. Don't worry, we'll have a good Christmas. I hope you are all well.

Don't worry, we'll be home in a couple of days. Don't think we don't miss you because we do.

I sure love you. Tell Virl, Tommy, Donny and Marie I love them too.

Love,

Wayne

way from Branson. But he always made a special effort to come to Mother and Father's for the holidays, and it made Christmas that much better.

Some of my children's favorite times were going over to Grandma and Grandpa's house on Christmas. It wasn't the presents—Mother, bless her heart, would usually give the grandchildren a church book. They cherish these books now, but at the time they would have rather had a squirt gun. (As a side note, Mother made some interesting gift choices. When I was eight, she wanted a girl so much that she gave all of her sons dolls for Christmas. Yuck!) Rather, my kids loved being able to hang out with their cousins; run wild through the backyard; and especially experience the love that they felt from their grandparents, uncles, aunts, and cousins. That love has kept our family strong, dedicated to each other, and itching for more family time together.

Jokes

Do you know what the favorite song at the schizophrenic ward is at Christmas time? "Do You Hear What I Hear?"

We were so poor the only thing I got for Christmas was a battery with a note saying, "Toy not included."

Chipmunks roasting in a forest fire.

I can't stand chess nuts boasting in an open foyer.

What do you call Santa's helpers? Subordinate Clauses.

The reason they have mistletoe hanging at the counters in airports is so you can kiss your luggage goodbye.

The Bermuda Triangle got tired of warm weather. It moved to The North Pole. Now Santa Claus is missing.

I told Santa Claus what I wanted for Christmas, and he said that he'd like that, too.

I gave my wife a gift certificate for Christmas. She ran out to exchange it for a bigger size.

Remember, hang on to your youth for as long as you can. The minute you stop believing in Santa Claus, you get socks and underwear for gifts.

The Christmas presents of today are the garage sales of tomorrow.

I don't mind getting money for Christmas; it's always just the right size.

For Christmas our dad got a puppy for Jay, and we all agreed that was a pretty fair trade for him.

I don't think I'll get my wife anything for Christmas this year. She still hasn't used the snow shovel I got her last Christmas.

I had a great Christmas. I received a lot of presents I can't wait to exchange.

I bought my son a bat for Christmas. On New Year's Eve it flew away.

This man's wife told him, "For Christmas, surprise me." On Christmas Eve he leaned over where she was sleeping and said, "Boo!"

Santa is having a heck of a time this year. Last year he deducted eight billion for gifts, and the IRS wants an itemized list!

If athletes get tennis elbow, what do astronauts get? Missile toe!

On Halloween, my parents used to send out Jay, as is.

The Little Men from Candy Land
Story written by George Osmond for his grandchildren
May 23, 1985; London, England

Once upon a time a long, long time ago, there lived in a small town a man and a woman and their two children. The father was a hard-working farmer. The mother was a housewife and a very good cook. The daughter was good to help her mother and kind to her little brother, Tim. It was customary for them to have a family get-together each Monday night and have a good, healthy meal, then a nice treat—as they did on this particular family night I am going to talk about.

This night the treats were beautiful, tasty, chocolate brownies. The mother placed five good-sized brownies on a plate in front of them—one for Father, one for Mother, one for big sister, and one for little Tim.

When they had finished and there was one left on the plate, the daughter said, "If I help you with the dishes, Mother, may I have the last brownie?"

The mother said, "Yes."

This made little Tim very unhappy, so he went to bed. Before going to sleep, he asked his mother if he could go and visit his grandparents who lived in the next town. Inasmuch as it would be Friday, he asked if he might stay over on the weekend and go see the carnival that was playing there. He would take the dollar he had in his bank and spend it all on candy—and get even with his sister for having the last brownie at dinner.

Next morning, his mother said he could go if he would be careful; so he took his dollar and went off to school. The bus ride to the next town would cost him thirty cents, so he decided to walk, instead, to save his money. In doing so, he became very tired. So when he saw a group of trees, he decided to stop and rest.

As he glanced around for a nice place to rest, he noticed a small building in the trees; so he went over and peered through the window. Inside was a strange metal ball with candy canes painted all over it.

"Well," he thought, "this must belong to the carnival." He became very curious, so he went into the building, walked up to the big metal ball, opened up the hatch, and climbed into it.

There were two little beds and a storage compartment in the back. The beds were very small, so he folded up his jacket for a pillow and lay down in back of them.

Pretty soon, the big door of the building was opened, and then the hatch; and there stood two little men. They had pointed noses, little yellow eyes, and their fingernails and toenails were also yellow. They had fat tummies and little round feet. They had sad faces, and their complexions were bad.

They climbed into the ball, and in seconds they were way up into the clouds. As they went through the last cloud cover, it shook the round spaceship, waking up little Tim.

He was so surprised that he just quietly lay and watched the many flashing lights on the panel in front of the little men. He watched them take candy bars out of their pockets and eat them, and drink from jars—orange, grape, lemon, and root beer soda (which seemed to be their favorite). Then they ate more candy bars and topped it off with ice cream bars.

They did leave one part of a candy bar on the seat in back of them; and because he was so hungry, Tim reached for it. They saw him and were so frightened, they just stared at him.

Finally, one of them spoke and asked him what he was doing there. Tim told them his story, and they smiled and hugged him, telling him that he was no doubt an answer to their prayers.

They told him that they came from the hollow earth country and that the health conditions in their country were very bad. They stated that many, many years ago they were normal people, but now they were deformed and sickly. They were on a mission to find someone that could help them.

This caused Tim to reflect on his training at home. He explained to them that his mother was a great cook and that she gave them good, hot, whole-grain cereal every morning. Only after family night dinner once each week did she give them a sweet treat.

Well, they took him into the hollow earth country, where they introduced him to their families. Later they took him back to his home to be with his mother, father and sister.

The father wanted to help them, also, so he gave them a baby boy calf and a baby girl calf to take home with them; also, some good foods to start them back on the road to health. In a few years they were healthy and smiling again—just like Grandpa's grandchildren.

Why did the pilgrims' pants always fall down? Because they wore their belt buckle on their hat.

What do you get when you cross an anesthesiologist with a rabbit? The Ether Bunny.

On Halloween, the parents send their kids out looking like me.

On Halloween, little girls get to dress up in Mommy's old clothes. Boys can't wear Daddy's old clothes, because Daddy's still wearing them!

When I was a kid I was so ugly my family had to celebrate Halloween every day just so I'd fit in!

14

Life and Living

A few summers ago, we ripped out a bunch of bushes to expand our driveway. The cement was laid, and all was going according to plan. Our neighbor was out on a walk and stopped to look at our cement. He had his dog walking alongside him, leashless. I knew what that dog was thinking—he wanted nothing more than to trample all over my newly laid, still-wet cement. Sure enough, he left his dirty little paw print in my cement, and we all watched him do it. "That's it—this is war!" I thought, as I stared the dog down.

By the cocky look that dog was giving me, I could tell that he would return to torture me. And I would be ready for him. The sun set, I whipped out my folding chair and BB gun, and I staked my claim next to the newly poured cement. With my arms folded and the gun laid across my lap, I was most definitely intimidating. I waited. Eventually, I laid down in the back of my car with the hatch opened, but I was still watching. Obviously, the dog thought I had let my guard down, so he finally pranced on by at around 3:00 A.M. to vandalize my cement once again. But, I didn't let him get away with it this time. As soon as I spotted him, I did all the yelling and chasing I could muster.

Obviously, he surrendered, and I was left with a couple slabs of flawless cement . . . at least until the neighbor kid rode a bike over the corner, some of my family members stepped in it, and the whole thing started to crumble within a year because it was a bad mixture of cement. So, we ripped it out and have only spent about five seconds thinking about it, since.

Life is kind of like that—we spend so much time trying to preserve what we have precariously built for ourselves (money made, prestige earned, career propelled), only to find out that what we have built is going to crumble, anyway. Lesson learned from this experience: life is too short to spend time worrying about cement. Instead, preserve the only things that won't wear out over time—your relationships. Which brings me to my next profound topic: video games.

Many a relationship has been built upon the strong foundation of video games. In fact, my brothers and I take our video games very seriously. When we were on the road in the late 70's and early 80's, we were guaranteed under contract to have access to video games backstage. At the very least, the contract required that there would be three different video games, one of which had to be Ms. Pac-Man. The other two needed to be Space Invaders and Pong, or suitable substitutes. No video games, no show. My brothers and I would play them for hours. They provided some mental distraction from the shows, spurred some competition, started some fights, and settled some disputes. Most of all, they kept us playing together.

I'm not quite so divalike about videogames now, but my family and I still love them. My daughter Sarah and I have especially bonded throughout our ongoing, ten-year Tetris tournament.

After I had my brain tumor removed, the doctors encouraged me to do something mentally stimulating every day in order to keep my mind active. I took that advice to heart and decided that Tetris was enough like a puzzle that it would be mentally stimulating. My daughter Sarah quickly joined in the fun. Sarah and I went back and forth for years trying to beat each other's score.

Though she was in college, she stopped by three or four times a week to check my high score, posted prominently on the refrigerator door. If I ever beat her, she stayed for the afternoon to regain her place at the top of the scoreboard. After she left, I immediately stopped

How to Save Time by Wayne Osmond
(written for English Composition in High School)

Time is the most valuable thing we have—far more precious than money or possessions. It is very easy to waste time; and when it is gone, there is no possible way of gaining any portion of it back. Therefore, I would like to suggest some ways I have found of saving time. . . .

A small notebook is the best method I have found for organizing time. My notebook is divided several ways. I have a section for "journal," one for "projects," one for "birthdays," "addresses," and phone numbers," etc.

One side of the journal is used to outline things I plan to do.

Each night the reverse side of the sheet is used to record what I actually accomplished. This serves as a check on myself. Things not accomplished will then be transferred to the next day's outline or to the "project" section.

I have used this system effectively for about six months. I can heartily recommend it to anyone.

what I was doing and played for hours (or days) until I had the high score once again. Sarah is currently in first place, but I'm only about 200 points behind. We're now in the 9,000-point range. (Kathy's score is 13; Michelle's is around 650.) Let's just say we're very dedicated to our game.

In 1978, we had just built our home in Provo, Utah. Alan and his family were building next door. The Osmonds were scheduled to perform at a grand opening of a resort, and it was publicized that the brothers and all of their families were going to spend several days there. But Amy and Steve were still babies and didn't travel well, so we decided to come home a few days early.

That night, Steve woke up, and Wayne went to the kitchen to make him a bottle. Steve fell asleep before Wayne could give him the bottle, so Wayne fell asleep on the couch waiting for Steve to wake up.

Suddenly, Wayne heard a loud "Bang!" Someone was trying to get into the house through the sliding door in the family room. He bolted down the hall to get his pistol and woke me up. We called the police to investigate the situation. The police came immediately and found a dent in the frame of our sliding door, where the burglar had tried to enter our house, probably thinking that it would be empty. I imagine the burglar was just as startled as Wayne was when Wayne jumped up from the couch and ran screaming down the hall!

—*Kathy, Wayne's wife*

Jokes

It's not the pace of life that concerns me, it's the sudden stop at the end.

If pro is opposite of con, is progress the opposite of congress?

Never say anything bad about a man until you've walked a mile in his shoes. By then he's a mile away, you've got his shoes, and you can say whatever you want to.

If you ever feel like dying, go to the living room!

Wasting time is an important part of life.

Work is for people who don't know how to fish.

Remember, work like a dog, eat like a horse, think like a fox, run like a rabbit, and visit your veterinarian twice a year.

Do you know what "dejamoo" is? It's the feeling you've heard this bull before.

Why take life seriously? You're not coming out of it alive, anyway.

How is it possible to have a civil war?

If you try to fail, and succeed, which have you done?

The earth is full—Go home.

Never hire an electrician without eyebrows.

One time a cop pulled me over for running a stop sign. He asked, "Didn't you see the stop sign?" I said, "Yeah, but I don't believe everything I read."

Rehab is for quitters!

The more people I meet, the more I like my dog.

I get enough exercise just pushing my luck.

Change is inevitable, except from a vending machine.

Ever stop to think and forget to start again?

A closed mouth gathers no feet.

Always remember you're unique, just like everyone else.

I'd give my right arm to be ambidextrous.

I'm not going to stand for this! So I sat down.

7th grade was the longest three years of my life!

Boy, you're a real lifesaver! I can tell by the hole in your head.

If it's true that we are here to help others, then what exactly are the others here for?

Today is the tomorrow you worried about yesterday, but not enough.

He who hesitates is probably right.

If you can smile when things go wrong, you have someone in mind to blame.

If at first you don't succeed, find out if there's a prize for the loser.

Nostalgia is longing for a place you'd never move back to.

Better get interested in your future. That's where you're going to spend the rest of your life.

The future isn't what it used to be.

It's hard to plan your future when you're busy repairing all the things you did yesterday.

If ignorance is bliss, why aren't there more happy people?

If at first you don't succeed, failure may be your thing.

If I didn't have hard luck, I wouldn't have any luck at all.

Maybe the trouble is we have ten million laws to enforce the Ten Commandments!

I had a terrible dream yesterday. I dreamed I was awake all night.

He was a responsible worker. If anything went wrong, they said he was responsible for it!

He discovered a new antiperspirant—unemployment!

When I was a kid, I would sometimes sneak out of my bedroom, go down the hall, and hide behind the couch in the family room to watch Dad play video games. When Super Mario 2 came out, Dad would play it for hours after we went to bed. One night, I was sneaking around and noticed that he was on the last level of Super Mario 2, so I had to watch and see if he finished the game. I was so excited when he won that I started to cheer. Dad, startled, turned around and saw me hiding behind the couch. But he was so excited that someone watched him win the game, he didn't care that I was out of bed. We just cheered together.

—*Greg, Wayne's son*

You can get more with a kind word and a kick in the rump than you can with only a kind word.

You can't believe everything you hear, but you can repeat it.

I found a surefire way of making my house look better. I go out and price new ones!

An insurance salesman sold me a great retirement policy. I gave him the first payment and he retired.

I tried to get a life insurance policy, but after a physical examination they offered me fire and theft!

He's got a great way of starting a day. He goes back to bed!

He missed his nap today. He slept right through it!

Considering the alternative, life isn't such a bad deal!

He is so unlike his echo which never comes back!

Most of the time people get what's coming to them—unless it's mailed!

One summer, Dad, Steve and I went on a three-week trip to California in a mobile home. The mobile home was great, until the night the bathroom stopped working. I had to go to the bathroom really badly, so Dad found an empty Squirt bottle and told me to relieve myself. Then we all went to bed. The next morning I was awakened by an "AAAGH!" Dad had woken up really thirsty and had been chugging "Squirt." He soon realized his mistake.

—*Greg, Wayne's son*

If at first you don't succeed, I suggest you don't play Russian roulette!

I'll give you an idea of how bad I am with plants. I fed a plant the other day, and it threw up!

You always get the last word if you argue alone.

Remember, if you have right on your side in a quarrel, that's important. If you have a two-by-four with a nail in it, that's not bad, either!

A good way to save face is to keep the lower half shut.

I live so far out of town, the mailman has to mail my letters.

Ambition is a poor excuse for not having enough sense to be lazy.

Change is inevitable, except from a vending machine.

Consciousness: that annoying time between naps.

Do unto others before they do it to you.

Do you always hit the nail right on the thumb?

Do it today—tomorrow it will be bad for your health or illegal.

Definition of "upgrade": Take old bugs out, put new ones in.

Don't judge a book by its movie.

Don't hate yourself in the morning: Sleep till noon.

Don't force it, get a larger hammer.

Don't take life too seriously, or you won't get out alive.

Don't wait: Postpone now!

Early to bed makes you healthy, wealthy and boring.

Eat one live toad the first thing in the morning and nothing worse will happen to you the rest of the day.

Every man has a scheme that absolutely won't work.

Everything going well? You must have overlooked something.

Everything is possible except skiing through revolving doors.

He who laughs last didn't get the joke.

He's turned his life around. He used to be depressed and miserable. Now he's miserable and depressed.

Help stamp out and abolish redundancy!

I don't know the secret to success, but the key to failure is to try to please everyone.

I sat down to daydream yesterday but my mind kept wandering.

I used up all my sick days, so I'm calling in dead.

I vow to live forever or die trying.

If everything is going well, you don't know what the heck is going on.

If it weren't for the last minute, nothing would get done.

In case of fire . . . yell "fire!"

It is no longer correct to call people "bald." They are "hairing impaired."

It's hard to fly with eagles when you work with turkeys.

It's not denial . . . I'm just selective about the reality I accept.

Junk: Something you need the day after you throw it away.

Jury: Twelve people who determine which client has the better lawyer.

For me kindness is like a boomerang—it always comes back.

Hey, boomerangs are coming back.

Laugh and the world laughs with you. Laugh at yourself, and they stare.

Life and liberty are safe only when Congress is in recess.

Loafer: Someone trying to make two weekends meet.

Look out for #1. Don't step in #2.

Maybe the grass is greener on the other side because there is more manure over there.

Men seldom show dimples to girls who have pimples.

Monday is an awful way to spend a seventh of your life.

Never delay the ending of a meeting or the beginning of a dinner hour.

No good deed goes unpunished.

No job is so simple that it can't be done wrong.

Nothing is as frustrating as arguing with someone who knows what he's talking about.

On the other hand, you have different fingers.

One good turn gets most of the blankets.

Never invite an arsonist to a housewarming party.

People who live in glass houses should get dressed in the basement.

Pessimist: An optimist with experience.

Practice makes perfect, but no one's perfect, so why practice?

Reality is for people who can't handle fantasy!

Reality is the only obstacle to happiness.

Shin: A device for finding furniture in the dark.

Short cut . . . the longest distance between two points.

Sometimes my tongue gets caught in my eyeteeth and I can't see what I'm saying.

Teamwork is vital . . . it gives you someone to blame.

The best thing about telling a clean joke is that there is a good chance that no one has heard it.

The drawback of being the toast of the town is that all the people are trying to butter you up.

Dad often liked to surprise us. One night, we were eating dinner in the kitchen and someone jumped up on the balcony and tried to open the sliding door. It really scared us all, especially because a burglar had once tried to break into our house by climbing onto the balcony. We were relieved to discover it was Dad, who had come home from tour a day early and wanted to make a big entrance. He definitely did!

—*Sarah, Wayne's daughter*

The greatest pleasure is doing what they said couldn't be done.

The length of a minute depends on which side of a bathroom door you're standing at.

The likelihood of a letter getting lost in the mail is directly proportional to its importance.

The pessimists answer to someone asking them how they are: "I'm fine, but I'll get over it."

The severity of the itch is proportional to the reach.

The simplest explanation is that it just doesn't make sense.

The problem with the rat race is that even if you win, you're still a rat.

The way to get to the top is to get off your bottom.

There is no substitute for good manners, except, perhaps, fast reflexes.

There is nothing wrong with chasing your dream . . . you might catch it.

Those who live by the sword get shot by those who don't.

Today is the last day of your life so far.

Two wrongs are only the beginning.

Unhappiness is in not knowing what we want and killing ourselves to get it.

When all else fails, read the instructions.

What's the difference between ignorance and apathy? I don't know and I don't care.

How many people work here? About half of them.

Live each day as if it were your last and someday you'll be right.

Never drop your contact lenses during tap dancing class.

If Americans throw rice at weddings, do the Chinese throw hot dogs?

If oxygen tarnishes silver, can you imagine what it does to our lungs?

What does a mummy do to unwind?

Whenever I wear a turtleneck, I feel like I'm being choked by a really weak person.

I was up all night thinking about this talk. Wouldn't it be ironic if this talk put you to sleep.

I'm not going to bore you with a long speech; I can do that with a short one.

The last time I made a speech there was a man in the audience snoring. I woke him and said, "How long have you been sleeping?" He said, "As long as you've been speaking."

I feel like I'm in a rut. Everytime I go to bed at night, I find myself just getting up again in the morning.

Friction is a drag.

We should have a way of telling people they have bad breath without hurting their feelings, "Well, I'm bored. Let's go brush our teeth." Or "I've got to make a phone call, hold this gum in your mouth."

I grew up in a neighborhood so rough, I learned to read by the light of a police helicopter.

My neighborhood is so dangerous, America Online won't even deliver email here.

Time's sure fun when you're having flies.

I went to a palm reader. She said, "You need a manicure."

My mind not only wanders, it sometimes leaves completely.

I've been on so many blind dates I should get a free dog.

Guy: Will you marry me?
Girl: No.
And they lived happily ever after.

My karma ran over your dogma.

Well, enough about me. Let's talk about you. What do you think of me?

Why is there always a mailbox in front of a post office?

A girl phoned me the other day and said, "Come on over, there's nobody home." I went over. Nobody was home.

That's a little known fact, because I just made it up.

What's happening? I give up. I'm no good at riddles.

What makes Teflon stick to the pan?

He slept like a log and woke up in the fireplace.

I told you a billion times not to exaggerate.

Words at a time like this are meaningless, so don't say anything.

The city just bought a new fire truck. The major says they'll use the old truck for false alarms.

If it works, don't fix it.

Experience: The name we give our mistakes.

I'm sorry I'm late, but my watch fell in the sheep dip and killed all the ticks.

All true wisdom is found on T-shirts.

Why is the third hand on the watch called a second hand?

Nobody's perfect, but you're abusing the privilege.

Women's Dictionary: Argument (ahr-gyuh-muhnt) n. A discussion that occurs when you're right, but he just hasn't realized it yet.

Women's Dictionary: Hairdresser (hair-dres-er) n. Someone who is able to create a style you will never be able to duplicate again. See also, "Magician."

If you can remain calm, you don't have all the facts.

Laughing helps. It's like jogging on the inside.

15

Money and Finances

Well, Kathy would be the first to tell you that managing money isn't one of my strengths. Luckily, she knows how to do all of that stuff, so she's nice enough to take care of everything for me. She's taught me a thing or two about finances through the years. For example, before we got married, I could use a credit card really well, but she had to teach me how to write a check. Now she's wishing she never showed me how to do that—I lose the checkbook a lot. Losing credit cards is another one of my specialties. I'm getting better, though—last year, I only had to cancel my credit cards four or five times.

When the economy is bad, we all need to hear jokes about our finanaces. Humor is cathartic—Aristotle described it a "purging" of emotions, which can also be translated as "a huge stress reliever." It helps us to laugh so we don't cry. So bring on the money jokes!

Jokes

I started out with nothing, and I still have most of it.

Despite the cost of living, have you noticed how it remains so popular?

I wished the buck stopped here, as I could use a few.

I went into the bank this morning and asked the teller to check my balance. So she pushed me.

Always live within your income, even if you have to borrow to do it.

Borrow money from a pessimist. They don't expect it back.

I saw a bank whose sign said, "24 Hour Banking," but I don't have that much time.

I took lessons in bicycle riding, but I could only afford half of them. Now I can ride a unicycle.

Did you ever notice that when you put the two words "the" and "IRS" together, it spells "THEIRS."

The company accountant is shy and retiring. He's shy a quarter of a million dollars. That's why he's retiring.

Old accountants never die. They just lose their balance.

Many people can't stand prosperity. Most don't have to.

It's hard to save your money for a rainy day, because it always keeps on raining.

A man said his credit card was stolen, but he decided not to report it because the thief was spending less than his wife did.

"Who should we pay first—the gas company or the doctor?" "The gas company. What can the doctor turn off?"

I just burned a hundred-dollar bill. It's easier to burn them than to pay them.

Times are so bad, stores are getting returns from shoplifters!

Things are so bad, I can put on my socks from either end!

I've saved up enough money to last me the rest of my life—unless I want to buy something!

There's an advantage to going broke. It's not expensive.

All you get when you pick my pocket is practice.

Times are bad when you go to the park and see the pigeons feeding people!

Times are tough when you open your refrigerator and a roach tries to pull you in.

Times are so bad, parents are writing to their kids in college to send money home.

Things are so bad, the mice only use my house for a shortcut!

I beat the recession last year. I went broke two years ago.

"I hear you're really going after the guy who robbed the bank, yesterday."
"You bet. If he wanted to steal, why didn't he work his way up in the bank like I did!"

"I'm here to speak to the loan arranger."
"He's not here."
"Well then, can I talk to Tonto?"

I must have a dishonest face. The bank asks me for identification when I deposit money!

"I was a cashier in a bank for a while, but then I went on to something else."
"What was that?"
"Jail!"

A young college grad applied for a job with a bank. The personnel officer asked, "What kind of job do you want?"

"I'll take vice-president for a start."

"We already have twelve vice-presidents."

"That's okay. I'm not superstitious."

A woman walked into a bank and said, "I want to open a joint account with somebody who has money!"

I just went partners with the bank. They own half of my car.

A woman walks into a bank to cash a check. The teller says, "You'll have to identify yourself." The man looks in the mirror and nods. "It's me, all right!"

If George Washington was such an honest man, why do they close the banks on his birthday?

"I wouldn't cash a check for my own brother."

"Well, you know your family better than I do!"

One bank opened a branch near a cemetery. In the window the president put a sign that read, "You can't take it with you when you go, but here's a chance to be near it!"

Jesse James told his brother Frank, "Tomorrow we rob the Second National Bank." Frank said, "We'd better not. That's where we keep our money!"

My wife makes the budget work. We go without a lot of things I don't need.

He's got a great way of saving money—he forgets who he borrowed it from.

He owes money that hasn't been minted yet!

Money may not be everything, but it sure keeps the kids writing to you!

There is only one problem with buying on time. When you get sick of something, you finally own it.

Every time my kid wants to quit school, I explain how important education is. If we couldn't sign our names, we'd have to pay cash!

Nowadays, if somebody pays cash, you worry that his credit is no good.

"How long will Fred be in Jail?"
"Thirty days."
"What's the charge?"
"No charge. Everything's free!"

The father said, "Young fellow, aren't you spending too much money on my daughter?" "Yes, sir," the young man said. "I wish you'd talk to her about that!"

"What should I do to keep from falling in love?"
"Try pricing houses!"

He has the first dollar he ever earned. He got it yesterday.

You have to give him a lot of credit. He has no cash.

I just started on my second million. I gave up on the first.

Work is a very unpopular way of making money.

I taught my son the value of a dollar. This week he wants his allowance in yen!

Gambling is a great way of getting nothing for something.

I know a fellow who makes only mental bets. The other day he lost his mind.

He comes from a moneyed family. His brother is worth fifty thousand, dead or alive!

The trouble is that when you don't pay your taxes in due time, you may do time!

The IRS has finally put poverty within our reach!

I feel great. I just paid my taxes, and I'm even for 1952!

Life insurance payments keep me broke, but there's a silver lining in that cloud—when I die I'll be rich!

I just signed for group insurance. If I die in a group, I get a hundred thousand!

I try to save my money. Who knows, maybe one day it'll become valuable again!

My brother has a great way of saving his money. He uses mine!

The pay clerk dropped Aggie's check on the floor by mistake and said, "I hope you're not afraid of germs."
Aggie said, "I'm not worried. No germ could live on what I make!"

If you want something that'll last forever, take out a mortgage!

I used to be bullish, then I was bearish. Now I'm brokish!"

If money is the root of all evil, then the stock market must be the Roto-Rooter!

I have a lot of "sweet chariot" stocks. The minute I buy them, they swing low!

Success is relative. The more success, the more relatives!

A penny saved is a Congressional oversight.

Budget: A method for going broke methodically.

Ever notice how the toast of the town is usually the person with the most bread?

We live on a dangerous fault—my income!

I wouldn't mind being poor if I had a lot of money.

IRS: We've got what it takes to take what you've got.

It's not hard to meet expenses; they're everywhere.

It's sweet to be remembered, but cheaper to be forgotten.

Crime doesn't pay and working for your boss doesn't, either.

I just bought a house I can afford. Now if I can just get it down out of the tree.

Remember, if you're late with your taxes the IRS will give you more time—like ten years!

I love those instructions on the back of the IRS envelopes. "Did you remember to affix your computerized sticker?" "Did you remember your W-2 forms?" "Did you remember to enclose the shirt off of your back?"

I just recently had my Visa card stolen. Right now it's everywhere I want to be.

I'm a writer. I write checks. They're not very good.

Money talks, although lately it's only been whispering.

All my money's tied up in poverty.

Sign posted: "A wallet was lost in the men's room. It was made of imported genuine leather. If found, you can keep the wallet, but please return the money, which was of sentimental value."

I'm so broke, I can't pay attention.

I dropped a dollar on the sidewalk and was arrested for littering.

They say money talks. Mine always says "good-bye."

This may not be a depression, but it's the worst boom we've ever had.

They called him "Bill," because he came at the end of the month.

Inflation is when the buck doesn't stop anywhere.

We were so poor that as kids, on Christmas Eve, we'd hang our stockings up, and the next morning they'd be nice and dry.

This guy is so cheap, he throws I.O.U.'s in wishing wells.

When I was a kid, I asked my dad for fifty bucks. He said, "Forty bucks! What do you want thirty bucks for?"

Bills travel through the mail at twice the speed of checks.

The cost of feathers is higher. That makes down up.

The Osmond Brothers

Osmond family when Marie was a baby (p. 97)

Olive, Wayne, and Merrill (p. v)

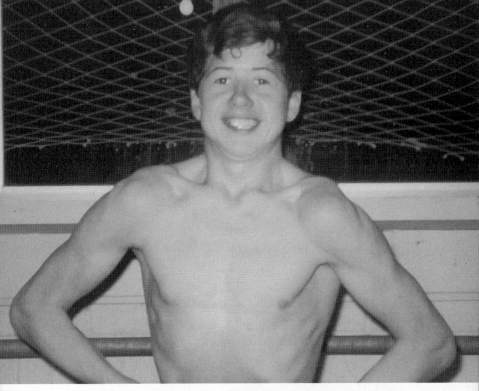

13-year-old Wayne flexing his muscles (p. 187)

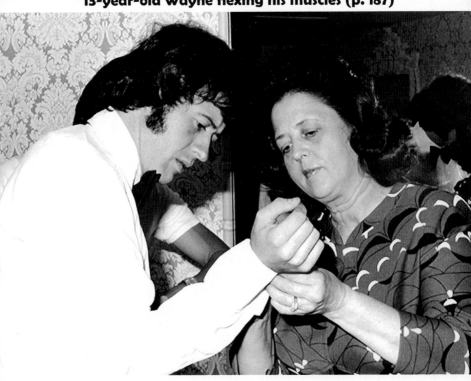

Olive helping Wayne before a show (p. v)

Wayne and Kathy on wedding day, Dec. 13, 1974 (p. 206)

Donny and Marie with handcuffs at wedding luncheon (p. 206)

Wayne and Kathy at wedding reception (p. 206)

Fixing a tire (p. 21)

The Osmond Brothers, featuring Jimmy

Saxophones on Thanksgiving, 1964

George and Wayne, 1977

Donny, Wayne, Merrill, Alan, and Jay

Osmond Brothers with Jerry Lewis, 1971

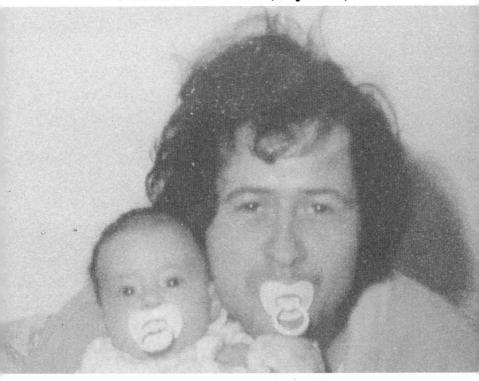

Wayne helping Amy stay pacified

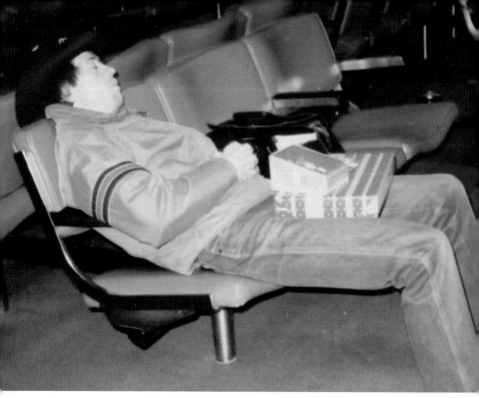

Wayne asleep at the airport

Steve caught a fish! (p. 199)

Provo, Utah home with Alan's yard next door (p. 2)

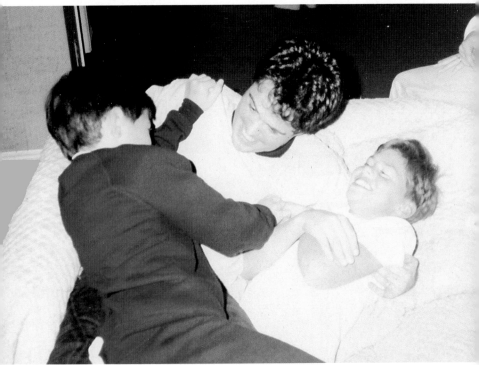

Steve and Greg tickling Donny (p. 97)

Jay, Merrill, Alan, and Wayne on a rollercoaster

Wayne loves to fly! (p. 92)

One of Kathy's favorite pictures of Wayne

Wayne recording

Target shooting with the orange Jimmy (p. 16)

Wayne's signature face

Dancing in Branson, MO, 1992

Telling "Rindercella"

Dancing in Branson

Teaching Amy to jump in Branson, 1993

Daisy, the Magic Pig (p. 1)

Playing the saxophone (photo by Sherry Croach)

Telling a joke

As an elf (photo by Sherry Croach)

Holding tired little Sarah

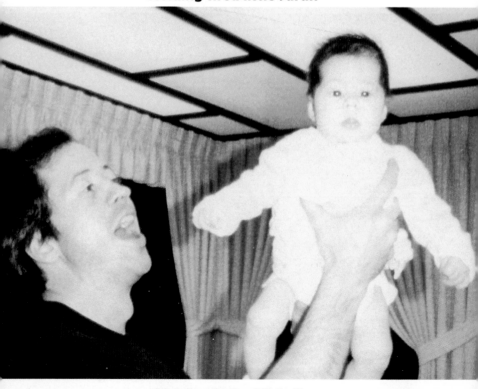

Holding baby Michelle

Wayne and his serious, well-behaved children

Noah with his grandpa's favorite drink (p. 77)

With Michelle in the Philippines (50th Anniversary Tour)

With Queen Elizabeth (photo by Doug McKenzie)

Oscar and his grandpa

Feeding the llamas (p. 5)

Sarah and Wayne: Tetris champions (p. 107)

Paul's famous leather belt (p. 185)

Marie teaching Wayne to sing classically (50th Anniversary Tour)

Kathy and Wayne singing in the rain in London

Guarding the cement (p. 105)

At Greg's graduation (p. 42)

Trying to beat Sarah at Tetris (p. 107)

Paul and Aili love Grandpa's ice cream parties! (p. 220)

So do Jacob and Maia! (p. 220)

16

Music and Show Business

Every show is different because every audience is unique. If you want to have a good show, you have to get to know the people in the audience and tweak your show to cater to them. So, how do you cater to an audience of hardened criminals? Good question.

A friend of our manager found himself in one of the California prisons. Our manager wanted us to go down and do a show for his friend and the rest of the inmates. I was a little apprehensive about the situation and had no idea what to expect, but I agreed.

At the beginning of the show, I got up on the stage and said, "Hey, it sure is good to be with you guys today!" I guess I came off to perky for them: "Ahh, *?*!*" they replied in unison. Never in my life had I heard such foul language (and I'm in show business!); I got so nervous that my knees actually buckled. I fell forward, face first, off the stage. Every guy in the building roared. They couldn't stop laughing. I was so embarrassed, but I didn't have any choice but to get back on stage. By that time, everyone was still laughing. The rest of the show went smoothly, and we were well-received by our audience. In fact, several of the inmates came up to us after the show and told us how much they enjoyed our performance. I guess a nice face-plant off the stage can really break the ice.

Not every show came off smoothly, however. In 1975, we planned a world tour and tried to come up with some new, creative ideas for our shows. In London, we hired a guy that had worked with the production of Peter Pan to set it up so Donny could fly across the whole colosseum. At the beginning of the concert, he flew across the whole audience and was on his way back to the stage before everyone realized what had happened. It was so unexpected, they didn't think about looking up. When the press reviewed the show, they said it was silly that Donny had flown out over the audience. Interestingly enough, Mick Jagger did the same thing at one of his concerts in London a couple of years later; by then, the press thought it was brilliant.

Jokes

Back in the '70's girls were banging on the door, but I wouldn't let them out!

A man came to my door and said he had come to tune my piano. I said, "But I didn't call you." He replied, "No, but your neighbors did."

He sings like a prisoner. Behind eight bars and always looking for the right key.

What do you call a song sung in an automobile?
A cartoon.

I play the harmonica. All I have to do is get my car going really fast and stick it out the window.

I'd tell you some jokes now, but you'd only laugh!

My wife asked me how long I was going to be gone on this tour. I said, "The whole time."

I know how to make pianos talk. They say, "Get your clumsy hands off me!"

You know we do a lot of cruise ships. In fact, we performed on the very first cruise ship—Noah's ark. Oh! They were animals!

Folks, this song used to be called "Torture in the Tepee or the Pain Was Intense."

And before that it was called, "In Her Eyes Was 'Yes, Yes,' but on Her Face Was No Nose."

How about, "Get off the Stove Granny, You're Too Old to Ride the Range."

The all-time favorite, "I Hope You're Living as High on the Hog as the Pig You've Turned Out to Be."

And my favorite, "When They Operated on Papa, They Opened Mama's Male."

"Don't Fence Me In," by Bob Wire.

"Get Away from the Screen Door, Granny, You'll Strain Yourself!"

"Get Out of the Wheat Field Granny, You're Goin' against the Grain."

A banjo is like an artillery shell—by the time you hear it, it's too late.

A saxophone is like a lawsuit. Everyone is happy when the case is closed.

What do you call a musician without a girlfriend? Homeless.

Do you know the definition for "perfect pitch?" When you throw the banjo into the dumpster and it lands right on the accordion.

What's the difference between an accordion and an onion? No one cries when you cut up an accordion.

What do you get when you drop a piano down a mine shaft? A-flat miner.

What's the difference between a banjo and a vacuum cleaner? You have to plug in a vacuum cleaner before it sucks.

How I Got into Show Business
(Wayne's High School English Paper)

Because of the belief in the talents of his grandkids, our Grandpa Davis paid to have a film made of us performing. He sent this film to Lawrence Welk as an audition medium because he wanted us to perform on the Lawrence Welk Show. Mr. Welk liked our film and invited us to come down to Las Angeles and audition.

So we all packed up in our father's Chevy pick-up truck with a camper on the back and headed for Los Angeles, California. When we arrived, Mr. Welk had to leave because of some emergency, so we didn't get our audition. We did get to meet the Lennon Sisters though. What a sweet bunch of ladies. We've all been good friends ever since. My father was disappointed but said, "What the heck. Let's go to Disneyland!" So we did!

How do you get a guitar player to turn down the volume? Put sheet music in front of him.

What's the difference between a viola and a coffin? The coffin has the dead person on the inside.

How does a guitar player make a million dollars? He starts out with seven million.

How many musician jokes are there? Just one—all the rest are true.

You've just been listening to that great Chinese speaker— On Too Long!

We had always dressed alike—Alan, Merrill, Jay, and myself. We noticed, singing on the streets of Disneyland, a barbershop quartet, The Dapper Dans. While they were singing, they noticed us listening to them and that we were dressed all alike just like them. They said, "Are you guys a group?"

We said, "We're a barbershop quartet just like you."

They said, "Sing us a song."

We did and then they would sing one and then we would sing a song. People started gathering around and stopping to hear us sing. They took us to their boss, Tommy Walker, who loved us and gave us a job singing on the streets of Disneyland for that whole summer. During that summer, Walt Disney made two of his "Disneyland After Dark" shows which included us. It was on those shows that Andy Williams' father saw us and asked us to come down to Los Angeles and audition for his son's new TV show. We did and we were with Andy for seven years.

A magician had a terrible accident while he was doing a trick that involved sawing his female assistant in half. The assistant left the act and moved to Dallas and Tulsa!

I'm as nervous as a mailman at a dog show!

Thank you for that wonderful round of indifference!

Never try to teach a pig to sing. You'll be wasting your time and bugging the pig.

She was a go-go dancer. Men looked at her face and said, "Go! Go!"

I'd be a great dancer except for two things—my feet!

Why do bagpipe players walk when they play? They're trying to get away from the noise.

What do you get when you play a country music song backwards? You get your wife back, your job back, your dog back . . .

What happens when a ghost haunts a theater? The actors get stage fright.

Dad is a stickler for arriving early to the theater before shows—often, he'll get there two hours early to prepare. But one time, Dad was running late to a show in Branson. He ran to the car only to realize that his keys were locked inside. He didn't have time to wait for a locksmith, so he took matters into his own hands. He punched a hole in the back left window, unlocked the car, fetched the keys, and headed off to the theater. I guess the show really must go on!

—*Greg, Wayne's son*

(When mike doesn't work) Can you hear me? I've spoken to more dead mikes than an Irish undertaker.

(When mike doesn't work) Aren't you glad our sound man doesn't make pacemakers.

(Sip from a water glass) Wow! I've gotta get that recipe.

(Someone sneezes) Wow! That one blew the monogram right off the handkerchief!

(Someone walks in late) Where have you been? You're lucky. I almost marked you absent.

(To a bearded man) Get a load of that beard! Were you born or trapped?

(Joke dies) That's the last time I'll ever buy a joke from _____.

(Joke dies) I practiced that joke in front of a mirror and got the same response.

(Joke dies) As my dad used to say . . . (Pause) Well, Dad didn't say much.

(Joke dies) If you found anything that I said this evening to be enlightening or beneficial, you need help!

(Joke dies) I've talked so much tonight, I think my lips have lost weight.

(Joke dies) My last audience gave me a nice basket of fruit—one piece at a time.

(Joke dies) That remark makes about as much sense as an ashtray on a motorcycle.

(Joke dies) Tonight's program was produced by Ronald Meedy and Jeremy Oaker. This has been a Meedy/Oaker production.

(Joke dies) We both drew straws to see who'd emcee, and my drawing looked least like a straw.

(Joke dies) We will now take a look at the instant replay so you can get a close-up look at that joke dying.

(Joke dies) As I said before, I never repeat myself!

(Joke dies) Are part-time band leaders semi-conductors?

(Joke dies) We'll be out of here faster than a fat kid in dodgeball.

(Joke dies) Here's another one you might not care for.

When a Chinese kid sits at the piano, does he play forks and spoons?

I'll remember this evening for as long as it takes me to get to my car.

I'm really happy to be here tonight. You know how fickle parole boards can be.

Next time you take a cruise, remember that you eat all the time, so take three outfits: large, extra large, and blimp.

Anybody in the audience with a New York license plate BL 758367458959473628474565783926102840284, will you kindly move it? Your license plate is blocking traffic.

(Flash picture) I think I just got flashed!

We went on a cruise for romance, but my wife and I found that by the time we got back to the cabin, we were so stuffed we were in pain. "OW, don't touch me." "I can't move, I want to die!" "What time is it?" "Midnight buffet?" "Let's go!"

I hate music, especially when it's played.

I don't know much about music. In my line of work you don't have to.

I used to like dancing, but the music would always throw me off.

Perhaps it was because Nero played the fiddle they burned Rome.

Once in a lifetime a really beautiful song comes along—until it does, I'd like to do this one.

I recently performed at an animal rights barbeque.

What is the difference between a bagpipe and an onion? Nobody cries when you chop up the bagpipe!

What's the difference between a lawnmower and a soprano sax? You can tune a lawnmower, and the neighbors are upset if you borrow a lawnmower and don't return it.

How do you make a chainsaw sound like a baritone sax? Add vibrato.

What's the difference between a dead snake in the road and a dead trombonist in the road? Skid marks in front of the snake.

When the Brothers decided to go country and get a new look, Dad decided to grow a mustache. He never did like it very much, though. One day I looked in the toilet and it looked like a mouse was in there. I then realized that my dad had shaved his mustache off.

—*Greg, Wayne's son*

What's the definition of a nerd? Someone who owns his own alto clarinet.

When he was a kid, Jay swallowed a harmonica. The doctor said, "It's lucky he wasn't playing the piano."

(Magic trick) Laugh, but it kept me out of the Army.

Last week, I performed at a Xerox convention and they made me do the same trick twenty times.

Remember, do it just like we rehearsed it—only good.

(After a weak introduction) I hope I can live up to that introduction.

About this next trick, I've had a request. I'm going to do it, anyway.

This trick was originally developed for an encore. But I never got to do it.

This trick has never been seen before on any stage. And for good reason.

This magic dust is invisible. Which makes it hard to find.

(For a heckler) Oh, someone from another planet.

It was nothing. I can tell by the applause.

So far, I'm not crazy about you, either.

Did I mention that the air conditioning system runs on applause (or laughter)?

That came out wrong only if you heard it.

It certainly is nice to be among friends . . . and I wish I were.

If this is boring you, just think how many times I've heard it.

(After little or no reaction) I know I'm here, I recognize my suit.

This section (point to one part of the audience) join hands. We'll try and contact the living.

Did I mention that I only have a few weeks to live?

What a nice quiet place to come and rehearse.

I thought I'd throw that in. Think I'll throw it out.

(To a heckler) Goofy's here tonight.

(To a hecker) What are you gonna be if you grow up?

I call 'em shissors, because I can't say scissors.

I worked on a lot of awful programs, er, an awful lot of programs.

And now I'll make the entire audience disappear (Blindfold yourself).

(After applause) Please don't stand, they'll think you're leaving.

I'd like to turn from varicose to a serious vein.

I know what's going on in your mind. I used to have one, myself.

(After doing something that leaves you out of breath) I'd like to do more, but the band is tired.

I'm pretty good at talking to people. I have the ability to uh, um, ah, adlib.

No applause! You're ruining my timing.

You've seen a lot of clever magic. I'm gonna put a stop to that.

I've often been accused—and sometimes convicted.

How many of you are here tonight?

Save your questions until after I've left.

That was unequalled, unrivalled, and unforgivable.

Most people take years to put their act together. Here's a guy that'll do it before your eyes.

I'm from the Performing Rights committee. You're not performing right.

Did you ever see me in the movies? I go quite often.

Before you say "Is that all there is?" that's all there is.

I've enjoyed about as much of this as I can stand.

Some acts are better than others. This act is one of the others.

He does bird imitations so well, I'm afraid to look up.

(After boring act) If you enjoyed that you're gonna love the rest of the show.

I'm here for comedy relief. I'm going to relieve you from comedy.

His new illusion is both good and original. But the part that is good is not original and the part that is original is not good.

He's brought happiness to literally dozens of people.

Somebody ill up there? Oh, that's your coat hanging over the rail.

(Stepping on mike cord) Oops, don't want to cut off my air supply.

He was on TV last week—interference.

You don't know him now. But don't worry, his face will grow on you. I'm glad it didn't grow on me!

The next act was going to be an escape artist but he got locked in his dressing room.

He began his distinguished career by singing—to a Congressional committee.

Once in a lifetime a great magician comes along. And while we're waiting, here's . . .

Was that an optical illusion or am I seeing things?

That's a lost art, and I can see why.

(Holding cloth) Here, clean up your act.

It could be called humorous. It could be, but . . .

He just returned from a week at the Frontier Hotel in Las Vegas, where he had a wonderful stay.

Would you mind standing a little closer to the floor?

(Selecting assistant) The lady in the blue yawning.

(After looking at the way someone is dressed) Unfortunately, this style will come back.

(After pointing to an unusual or loud garment) Are you wearing this on purpose?

How many of you are enjoying the show? (Some hands raised) How many of you don't like to raise your hands?

He thrilled thousands of Californians by moving to New York.

In the men's room there's a sign that says "Wet Paint." That's for information, not instruction.

I'm referring to my notes. (Hold up sheet of paper with giant musical notes on it.)

That music goes straight to my heart, and it's not doing my stomach any good, either.

(After looking at the band) No show would be complete without a great band. That's why we have an incomplete show.

The orchestra eats, sleeps, and reads music. If they could only play.

(To someone walking in late) You're late, did you bring a note?

(To man with mustache) You kiss a girl and give her the brush off at the same time.

(To a musician) Have you selected a career, yet?

I knew Mary when her hair was really that color.

(To a person sitting alone) Sitting with all your friends I see.

Marcel Marceau tells better jokes than you.

I won't bore you with a long speech; I'll leave that to our speaker tonight.

It's 10 o'clock. Do you know what time it is?

Observational humor is what I strive for, but I'll stoop to anything.

If I can make just one of you laugh . . . I'm in trouble.

It's nice to be looking into your faces. Some of your faces need looking into.

Paging Al Bino.

I've had lunch at the White House. Actually just crackers as I followed the guide.

This trick wowed 'em in New York. It wowed 'em in Chicago. In fact, it's the wowsiest trick around.

I don't do anything, but I do it well.

Save your applause. I have a weak finish.

(Small audience) I've seen more people on the back of a motorcycle.

I'm laughing at the next joke 'cause I know it.

This next act is called "Hope and Charity"—I have no faith in it!

He keeps doing it until he gets it wrong.

He can make people laugh any time he wants to. For the past ten years he just didn't want to.

You were never funnier and it's a shame.

Is there no beginning to your talent.

When you go home tonight, please drive on the sidewalk. All the accidents are happening in the street.

(After good, young performer) There are two things I hate: youth and talent.

I hope you'll enjoy it. You might as well.

If you've heard this one before, don't stop me 'cause I wanna hear it again.

Make your mind blank. That was quick!

Just stand on the red X. (There isn't a red X, but they will look for it.)

(To a man wearing sunglasses) Are you a pop star or a welder?

Blow on it. No, don't spit . . . it'll rust. (As a reward, feed the spectator as an animal trainer would reward a monkey.)

(After assistant has given her name) What is your first name Judy?

Too early to smile, huh?

Is this your first time in public?

Have we ever met before? ("No.") You seem happy about that.

Seymour (or another unusual name), they named you after—a long debate.

(As woman assistant comes up on stage) Is that your husband with you? You don't look happy about it.

That's a searsucker suit and he's the sucker that bought it at Sears.

I crossed an alligator with a skunk. I got shoes no one would wear and a purse no one would open.

(To person wearing checked or plaid suit) Nice coat. Did you get a chess set with it?

(About coat) What a lovely shade of tweed.

That's a great outfit . . . if you're a flag.

(To a man wearing a jacket and slacks, different colors): What's the matter? Couldn't you decide which suit to wear?

Before I speak, I wanna say something.

He plays fourth trumpet in a trio.

George: When I left the stage, the audience went
           wild with applause.
Harry: That's because they knew you weren't
           coming back.

We've got a three-piece group here. We only know three pieces.

I loved the big sign that said, "Welcome, Wayne Osmond." I was so embarrassed, though . . . they caught me putting it up.

We've appeared all over the world, before the Queen of England, The Grand Shah of Iran, Next we're going to Washington to appear before the Grand Jury.

Come on folks, it's not easy getting up in front of people and speaking like this. What you have to do is go to diction school. Now, at diction school they teach you how to speak clearly and properly and they fill your mouth full of marbles. You speak right through the marbles. Every day you lose one marble. Now when you've lost all your marbles, then you're qualified to be an entertainer.

"Where did you learn to sing?"
"Oh, in the shower."
"You should have taken more showers."

As a singer I'm really worth watching. Too bad I'm not worth listening to.

Did anyone lose a roll of ten dollar bills in a rubber band? Well, I've got the rubber band, so just come and see me after the show.

Some acts are good, some acts are lousy; mine is good and lousy.

17

Places and Their People

When we're out on the road, there's a lot of waiting around. We wait to get there. We wait for call time. We wait for sound check, for dinner, for the show to start, and then we wait to go home. So, how do I pass the time while I'm waiting for it all to happen? By making bullets. Well, at least that's what I did back in the 70's. We'd stop at the gas stations and they'd have scraps of old lead there. I'd go beg the lead off of them, and I could usually coax them into giving it to me. Then, I'd use it to make bullets. I had this suitcase that I would lug my bullets around in while we'd travel from place to place.

One day my family and I were headed up to Canada to do a show. We took a plane, while the band and crew drove a bus loaded with all of the equipment over the Canadian border. I had left my suitcase filled with bullets on the bus since it weighed about 400 pounds, which exceeded the weight limits for an airline carry-on luggage item, even in the 70's. I was sure to lock the suitcase too. I didn't want anyone messing with my bullets!

When the customs officials came across my laden, locked suitcase, they were skeptical of the band and crew. Our guys tried and tried to explain to them how I collected lead and made bullets, but what idiot is going to believe a tale like that? And even if they believed it, why would they let a bus full of bullets into Canada? The officials tried to break the lock on the suitcase to put an end to the stories, but they couldn't open it. They had no choice but to detain the bus and crew for 14 hours on the U.S. side of the Canadian border due to that one little four hundred-pound piece of suspicious luggage. Oops.

Jokes

Do people in Australia call the rest of the world "up over?"

Welcome to Utah; set your watch back 20 years.

What do Eskimos get from sitting on the ice too long? Polaroids.

The last time I went to Canada I went to a fight and a hockey game broke out.

The last time I went to Wisconsin; I got locked up. I didn't go to jail, I just ate too much of their cheese!

You're from Illinois. Are you ill or annoyed?

How is a divorce in North Dakota like a hurricane in Florida? Either way, you lose the trailer.

A mine owner advertises for new workers and three guys turn up: an Irish man, an Italian, and a Japanese man. The owner tells the Irish man, "You'll be in charge of the mining." He tells the Italian, "You'll be in charge of the lift." He tells the Japanese man, "You'll be in charge of making sure we have supplies." The next day the three men go into the mine, and at the end of the day one man is missing, the Japanese man. They search for him for hours. Just as they are about to give up, he jumps out from behind a rock yelling, "Supplies! Supplies!"

What's the difference between a Utahn and a canoe? A canoe will sometimes tip.

A mind reader relocated to California. In two weeks he almost died because he had nothing to do!

There may be other cities in England foggier than London, but it's hard to tell which they are, because of the fog.

Florida hurricanes aren't all bad. The other day, my car got two hundred miles to the gallon!

At a Hawaiian luau they eat with their fingers. I have a family at home like that!

A visitor in Houston asked, "What's the fastest way to the hospital?" A local said, "Say something bad about Texas!"

You know you're in Los Angeles when you put air in your tires and they cough!

A census taker asked an Ozarkian, "What's your birthday?" The Ozarkian said, "February 8." "Which year?" "Every year!"

Crime is so bad in our country that the Statue of Liberty started holding both hands up in the air.

My home state is so poor, our electric chair is a wind-up!

The San Andreas fault is the most stable thing in California.

What city has the largest rodent population? Hamsterdam.

The town was so small it said, "Welcome to _____" on both sides of the sign.

The town is so small it only has one bumper car.

Polynesia: Memory loss in parrots.

Show me an Eskimo who sells eyeglasses and I'll show you an optical Aleutian.

We were in New York picking up shells on the beach—22 shells, 45 shells, 38 shells, shotgun shells . . .

In Los Angeles, pollution is so bad I put air in my tires and two of them died.

Do people from Belgium speak Belch?

You're from Dixie? I use your cups.

It was so smoggy in Los Angeles I inhaled and chipped a tooth.

It was so smoggy in Los Angeles I shot an arrow into the air and it stuck.

He's from New York. He used to run five miles a day—three for his health, two for his life.

Last week, the wind stopped blowing in Chicago, and everyone fell down.

It's a great community if you own a gun.

Buffalo. It's not the end of the world. But you can see it from there.

What kind of shoes do lazy people wear? Loafers.

Well, I've been traveling a lot lately. I just got back from Mexico where I was performing at the Kaopectate festival down there. Had to make a run for it.

(After asking someone where they are from) Oh! That's a good place to be from . . . far from.

(After finding out where someone was from) I spent four years there one night.

What's round on both sides and high in the middle? Ohio.

18

Psychiatry

My brothers have always thought I was a little different. You don't get the nickname "Crazy Wayne" for nothing. I have done all sorts of questionable things, like leaving my groceries at the store after buying them; going on a month-long world tour with only one set of underwear (which I washed every day, thank you very much); and sticking straws up my nose and in my ears while eating by myself at Wendy's to see whether people would notice. But the following incident had my brothers ready to send me to the funny farm.

Once I was on tour and decided to take a nap before the evening show. I locked the deadbolt on the door for security, took out my hearing aids, and fell into a pretty deep sleep. Eventually, I was awakened by a soft "tap, tap, tap" sound. I went to the door to see who it was. It was the hotel manager and some of the workers getting ready to break down my door. I quickly realized that I had overslept and was almost late for my show; so Merrill and Jay, who were already at the venue, had asked the hotel staff to try to wake me up. The hotel workers had been calling my phone and pounding on my door for quite some time. They had even brought up a security guard to try to unlock my door. They were just about to move on to the last possible course of action—breaking down my door—when I finally woke up. I awoke just early enough to get dressed, drive to the venue, and walk on stage. After this mishap, Kathy bought me an alarm clock called "the Sonic Bomb" that vibrates and has flashing lights. It's made to wake up deaf people.

Jokes

Doctor said, "You're crazy." I said, "I want a second opinion." He said, "Okay, you're ugly too."

A man consults a therapist and states, "Doc, I'm suicidal. What should I do?" The doctor replies, "Pay in advance."

I said, "Doc, Can you cure me?" He said, "Not on your salary."

I went to the doctor the other day and I said, "Doc, I've got a problem! I think I'm a moth!" He said, "a moth— well you don't need to see me, you need to see a psychiatrist!" I said, "I was on my way there when I saw your light on."

I went to my shrink the other day and I said, "Doc, I'm schizophrenic." He said, "that makes four of us!"

Roses are red, Violets are blue, I'm Schizophrenic, Hey! So am I.

I went to my Shrink and I said, "Doc, I'm schizophrenic; but, it's OK, I have each other!"

How do crazy people go through the forest? They take the psycho path.

I don't suffer from insanity, I enjoy every minute of it.

I'm in my own little world. But it's OK—they know me here.

I remember I was so depressed I was going to jump out a window on the tenth floor, so they sent a priest up to talk to me. He said, "On your mark . . ."

When I'm feeling down, I like to whistle. It makes the neighbor's dog run to the end of his chain and gag himself.

I do whatever my Rice Krispies tell me to.

You're just jealous because the voices only talk to me.

When I'm not in my right mind, my left mind gets pretty crowded.

What lies at the bottom of the ocean and twitches? A nervous wreck.

The sky is falling . . . no, I'm tipping over backwards.

I like to torture my plants by watering them with ice cubes.

Ever stop to think and forget to start again?

Olive Osmond

When Wayne was about 2 ½ he had an imaginary friend named Joe Anson (not Hanson). This "friend" would tell him all kinds of things. When we'd question him, he'd simply remark, "That's what Joe Anson told me."

There are three kinds of people: those who can count and those who can't.

"Hello? Is this the state mental hospital?"
"Yes it is."
"Can I speak to Mr. Russell in room twenty-seven?"
"One moment and I'll connect you (pause). I'm sorry, Mr. Russell's not answering."
"Good. That means I must have really escaped."

One absentminded gent slammed his wife and kissed the door good-bye.

Talk about an absentminded man—yesterday he cut his finger and forgot to bleed!

The ladies can be flaky too. A very pretty lady had the kind of charms that would smite a man. In this case, one of the smitten asked, "Could I have your phone number?" The pretty lady said, "It's in the telephone book." "Great! What's your name?" "Oh, that's in the phone book too!"

If ignorance is bliss, he's Mr. Happy!

The other day an idea went through his head. There was nothing to stop it.

He changed his mind the other day. The new one doesn't work any better!

He says he's got an open mind, but it's really vacant!

He'd give you a piece of his mind, but it's not big enough to subdivide.

They named a town in Massachusetts after him— Marblehead!

He's so dumb, he'd look through a peephole with his glass eye.

He's not a genius. When the power went out, he was stuck on the escalator for two hours.

One mobster wasn't too bright. They asked him to blow up a truck. He burned his lips on the exhaust.

I subscribe to a science-fiction magazine: "Better Homes and Gardens."

"They call him 'Peanut Brittle.'"
"Why?"
"Because he's half nuts!"

"Does he suffer from insanity?"
"No, he enjoys every minute of it!"

They call her "Venus de Milo" because she's not all there!

I spent two years in an asylum. I was crazy about the place!

The psychiatrist had a tremor in his voice as he told Mr. Cooper, "I regret that I have to tell you this—your wife's mind is gone." Mr. Cooper said, "I'm not surprised. She's been giving me a piece of it every day for twenty years!"

The psychiatrist examined ten-year-old Willie and told his mother, "Mrs. Bronson, you need some help, too. You're too concerned and nervous about your son. I'll give you some tranquilizers that you'll take regularly until I see you next week." The following week, the Bronsons returned. The psychiatrist asked, "How's Willie?" Mrs. Bronson said, "Who cares?"

"Doctor, I just can't stop believing I'm a dog."
"How long has this been going on?"
"Since I was a puppy!"

One thing about stupidity is that you can be pretty certain it's real!

A patient says, "I think I'm an umbrella."
The psychiatrist says, "A cure is possible if you'll open up."
The patient says, "Why? It is raining?"

There's a good reason he has a stupid look on his face—he's stupid!

He doesn't buy toothpaste because his teeth aren't loose!

When he got out of kindergarten he was so excited he could hardly shave!

One out of every three people in the United States is mentally ill. Look at the person on your left and on your right. If they're OK, it's you!

A drunk man walked over to a man and asked, "Do you have the time?" The man said, "Eight-fifteen." The drunk man said, "I think I'm going nuts. All day long I've been getting different answers!"

Olive Osmond

One day in the car we were just getting ready to go home from my father's place. Wayne said, "Grandpa, you're a mental case." It about floored us all. He'd heard that expression on the Jackie Gleason Show on TV.

Brains aren't everything. In his case they're nothing!

Everyone hates me because I'm paranoid.

I am not a complete idiot; some parts are missing!

I can see clearly now, the brain is gone.

I don't have a solution but I admire the problem.

In some countries, "fundamentalist" is just a fancy name for a nutcake with explosives.

Mental block: A street on which several psychiatrists live.

Never argue with an idiot. Someone watching might not be able to tell the difference.

Remember: Lefties are the only people in their right minds.

Schizophrenia beats being alone.

The more stupidity you put up with, the more stupidity you are going to get.

People think he's a wit. They're half right!

I bought a book on obsessive compulsive disorders. It's great! I've already read it 523 times.

How many kids with ADD does it take to change a light bulb? Hey, Let's ride bikes!

Clara: Imagine meeting you here at the psychiatrist's office. Are you coming or going?
Maria: If I knew that, I wouldn't be here!

Morris went to a psychiatrist. "Doc," he said, "I'm going crazy. Every time I get into bed, I imagine there's somebody hiding under it."

"Just give me three years at three sessions a week and I'll have you cured," said the shrink. "How much do you charge?" asked Morris. "A hundred dollars per visit." Morris thanked him and left.

Six months later the doctor ran into Morris on the street. "I remember you. You're the fellow who kept imagining someone under his bed. Why didn't you ever come in for treatment?" asked the psychiatrist. Morris replied, "Because a bartender cured me for ten dollars." The psychiatrist was astounded. "How'd he do that?" Morris answered, "He advised me to saw the legs off the bed."

Insanity is hereditary; you can get it from your children.

"What does the cook in an insane asylum do?"
"He serves soup to nuts."

(After strange occurrence) Must be a full moon . . .

I just made two pictures. One like this (Turn sideways) and one like this. (Face front)

Raise your hand if you believe in ESP and powers of thought transmission. The rest of you turn around and see where all the nuts are.

The doctor cured his mental illness. He no longer thinks he's Napoleon. Now he's a nobody.

Anyone who goes to a psychiatrist ought to have his head examined.

He lost a thousand dollars playing solitaire.

His wisdom tooth is developmentally delayed.

He won a Gold Medal and was so proud he had it bronzed.

The Warning Signs of Insanity

You write to your mother in Germany every week, even though she sends you mail from Iowa asking why you never write.

Your breath smells more and more like squirrel dung each passing day.

You laugh out loud during funerals.

Nobody listens to you anymore, because they can't understand you through that scuba mask.

You begin to stop and consider all of the blades of grass you've stepped on as a child and worry that their posterity are going to one day seek revenge.

You have meaningful conversations with your toaster.

You collect dead windowsill flies.

You hear voices and know that it is the people in your shoes.

You offer to help the baggers at the grocery store and spend hours bagging groceries.

You hold conversations with your coffee pot in the morning and shout at the toaster for butting in.

You complain that silly string is really neat but it is nearly impossible to sew with.

He has an indoor windmill.

He just finished his first book. Next week he's going to read another one.

He told everyone he was a mute.

Here's a piece of advice: If you ever get amnesia . . . Why should I tell you? You'll forget, anyway.

If our knees bent the other way, what would chairs look like?

What's up? Certainly not your IQ.

She got mad at her plants. Now she's talking to the canned vegetables.

What's at the top of a moron's ladder? A sign that says "Stop."

Sign on psychiatrist's window: "50% off for half wits."

He can recite the alphabet clear up to one hundred.

You better start mixing toothpaste with your shampoo; you're getting a cavity in your brain.

A: I feel stupid
B: You look natural

A: You have your shoes on the wrong feet.
B: They're the only feet I have.

If you keep your head when everyone else is losing theirs, you'll be taller.

I know what's going through your mind. I used to have one, myself.

He was going to commit suicide by taking 500 aspirin. But after he took two, he felt better.

He's a man who's not afraid to say what he thinks—whether he's thinking or not.

Do you know why you weren't born smart? Because you were born dumb.

You look like you're posing for a postage stamp.

He can open envelopes with his breath.

A: You've got the brains of an idiot!
B: You want them back?

What makes him tick? And what makes him cuckoo every half hour?

She is on a wavelength with garage doors.

It's always great to meet a man that's not a credit to his race.

He has a clean mind . . . It's never been used.

He doesn't act stupid. It's the real thing.

He got stuck on an escalator in a blackout.

19

Put-Downs

Let's face it: we all love a good zinger, as long as it's not about us. Although I have been collecting put-downs for decades, I have received many more put-downs than I have ever dished out. I've even been put down in Russian. Well, sort of.

During the Cold War, we were on a flight home from Japan and stopped in Moscow to refuel an old DC-8 Stretch Mainliner. Upon landing, the plane hit the runway extremely hard and bounced to the right. We thought the plane was going to crash on its side, but the pilot managed to straighten it out. The plane then slammed down really hard again before it came to a screeching halt. It was the worst landing I've personally experienced. After getting off of the plane I went inside the airport to wait and sat down in a chair. I looked up and facing me were several Russian generals sitting in chairs. I was wearing my favorite light navy jacket with white stars and bold red stripes. The Russian general sitting across from me glared with disgust, put his hand up, and gave me a thumbs down—which he held down for quite a while. This made me uncomfortable, and a little nervous, so I decided to find a friendlier place to sit.

In my opinion, a put-down should only be used in a contrived situation with a willing opponent. A comedy roast is a perfect example. I also approve the use of any of the following put-downs on my brothers. If you're coming to one of the shows and want to use one, just email me and I'll let you know which of my brothers is bugging me most that day!

Jokes

Never underestimate the power of stupid people in large groups.

Light travels faster than sound. This is why some people appear bright until you hear them speak.

He who laughs last, thinks slowest.

She's such a bad cook, the family dog barks, "Barf, barf!"

She makes dehydrated food without adding water. The other day I went out in the rain and gained sixty pounds.

She couldn't get a date on her tombstone!

She's not popular. One day somebody took her out and left her there.

People like to help him out—as soon as he comes in!

His hosts like to see him to the door—a soon as possible!

All things being equal, you lose.

You know how you can tell if you are built upside down? Your nose runs and your feet smell.

I like your approach . . . let's see your departure.

I'd explain it to you but your brain would explode.

The wheels are turning, but the hamster's asleep.

Body by Nautilus, brain by Mattel.

In all fairness, my brother does have a photographic memory. He's just out of film.

My parents sent Jay to summer camp. My parents told him to put on a new pair of socks every day. When he came back, he was a foot taller.

Jay, shouldn't you be at the airport, sniffing luggage?

Once, as a boy, my brother started keeping a hamster in our room. At first, the smell was terrible, but the hamster got used to it.

Remember, if the shoe fits, get another one just like it.

If you're too open-minded, your brains will fall out.

How can I miss you if you won't go away?

Don't worry about what people think; they don't do it very often.

If walking is so good for you, then why does my mailman look like Jabba the Hutt?

The gates are down, the lights are flashing, but the train just isn't coming.

He keeps a coat hanger in the backseat in case he locks the keys in his car.

There's a bus leaving in a few minutes; please be under it!

It's one of those bands that make you want to stamp your feet . . . all over them.

Sorry, I don't date outside my species.

He looks like an unmade bed!

She's not photogenic, especially in person!

He just went on a crash diet. That's why he looks like a wreck.

She's not all here, and everybody's grateful!

He's such a miserable specimen it looks as if he was made in Hong Kong!

He'd make a great death wish!

His picture is in the dictionary under "Slob."

When he goes to a wax museum, he has to have a note to get out.

He clicks with everybody he meets. His dentures don't fit!

She was so ugly when she was born, for six months her folks diapered the wrong end.

She was so ugly, when she was born the doctor slapped her mother.

His parents spent a year looking for a loophole in his birth certificate.

When she was born, they didn't know whether to buy a crib or a cage!

People looked at her and wondered where the organ grinder was.

He's the son his father never had.

He was an only child, and he still wasn't his father's favorite.

He lights up a room by leaving it.

When he was born, his father went around showing people the kid's picture that came with the wallet!

When he was born, two nurses jumped on chairs.

He was so unpopular they had to tie a pork chop around his neck so the dog would play with him.

When she was a kid, her mother had to buy her back twice a week from the dogcatcher!

He was pretty dumb. He didn't know he was twelve until he was fourteen.

When they took him to the zoo, they needed two tickets for him—one to get in and one to get out.

Her family had a pet name for her because she looked like one.

She was so fat as a child, when she got off a merry-go-round the horse limped.

That's a nice suit. When did the clown die?

He could go on color TV and come out in black and white.

He's not the sharpest knife in the drawer!

He is such a dull guy, when he wakes up from a nap, there's a tag on his toe.

He's so dull he could be the poster boy for brown.

He always walks into a room voice-first.

You can count his enemies on the fingers of the Mormon Tabernacle Choir!

He'd give you a penny for your thoughts, and we all know what animal gives a scent!

He was a member of the human race, but he was dropped.

She was so cross-eyed she could look through a keyhole with both eyes!

To give you an idea of her looks—on her face she had a beauty question mark!

She had her face lifted, but it didn't help. There was another one just like it underneath.

She went to the beauty parlor the other day, begging for one last chance.

His face looks like his hobby is stepping on rakes!

Somebody ought to give him a fat lip so it would match the rest of him!

Her feet were so big, her toes had to get their own shoes!

Her feet were so big she was often rented to stamp out forest fires!

Nobody likes him. He brought a parrot home and it told him to get out.

A woman rushed after the garbage truck and asked, "Am I too late for the garbage?" The collector said, "No, jump in!"

She's so unpopular she used to go to Lover's Lane and try to pick up a cop!

She wanted to see something in fur, so her boyfriend took her to the zoo.

His mouth is so big he can whisper in his own ear!

You have a lot of get-up-and-go. Please do!

Don't fall on your head. It'll knock you conscious!

Please throw your hat away, but leave your head in it!

He can't be two-faced, or he'd be wearing the other one!

He's got a hole in his head, but that's beside the point!

How can people miss him if he won't go away?

People like to hate him in installments so it will last longer!

He leaves a bad taste in people's eyes!

I understand that you are kind to inferiors. Where do you find them?

If this guy had greatness thrust upon him, he'd ask if it came with directions!

One habit gives her away. She likes to nip at strangers' heels!

Every time she wants to express herself, people suggest UPS!

He lives on the wrong side of a one-track mind!

He never did a thing in his life, and he didn't do that well!

He'd give away the shirt on his back. The Board of Health would insist on it!

He's a man who started at the bottom and sank!

To him, bubble-gum cards are part of the Great Books series!

Her mouth is big enough to sing duets!

The other night he was down in the dumps. That's where he lives!

His name must be "Theory," because he never works!

The secret of his success still is!

He's not a bookworm, just an ordinary worm!

He has no hang-ups. Everything he owns is on the floor!

If his IQ were any lower, he'd trip over it!

She has a walk-in mouth!

He's got as much future as a cake of ice!

You have a wonderful head on your shoulders. Whose is it?

He looks like he finished last in the human race!

She didn't look like an old maid. She looked more like an unmade!

Men always wanted her hand in marriage, but the problem was that they had to take the rest of her, too!

Her teeth were like stars. They came out at night!

Your train of thought, sir. Does it have a caboose?

I love that formal wear. I didn't know Fruit of the Loom made tuxedos.

I saw a teenager who had a ring in her nose, a ring in her eyebrow, and a stud through her tongue. She looked like she had fallen face-first into a tackle box.

He was so ugly my parents used to sit him in the corner and feed him with a slingshot.

I've known him all my life, but it seems longer.

When he was born, his parents snuck out of the hospital with bags over their heads.

We were going to put a statue of him in the park, but then we figured, why should we scare the poor pigeons?

When they made him they threw away the mold, but it appears to be growing back again.

He's been called a self-made man, which just shows what can happen when you don't read the instructions.

He's so dumb he thinks Taco Bell is the Mexican phone company.

He's so dumb. His wife asked him to change the baby and he brought home a different kid.

Have you ever been to the zoo? I mean as a visitor.

He's not an only child, but his mom said that if he had been born first he would have been.

I've heard a lot about him, and someday I'd like to hear his side of the story.

Men like him don't grow on trees; they usually swing from them.

She is so skinny that when she takes a shower she has to wear skis so she won't go down the drain.

He believes a friend in need is a friend you stay away from.

I hope you're living as high on the hog as the pig you turned out to be.

She's so ugly that the waiter in the restaurant put her plate on the floor.

May I borrow your nose? I need to open a pop bottle.

She's so ugly that if she moved next door to you, your lawn would die.

Don't look now but there's a dummy standing in your shoes.

Why don't you take lockjaw lessons.

I'd like to help you out. Which way did you come in?

Don't think it hasn't been a pleasure to meet you . . . because it hasn't.

She only lies when she speaks.

He's got insomnia and is trying to sleep it off.

Was it you or your brother who died?

He's so tough he can make a fist with his nose.

He thinks he's a chicken. But we don't try to talk him out of it, because we need the eggs.

His idol is President Rushmore.

It's people like you that make me hate people like you.

I had a nightmare last night. You were it.

If you ever need a friend, buy a dog.

What's on your mind, if you'll forgive the understatement.

A: Are you afraid of the big bad wolf?
B: No.
A: Funny, the other two little pigs were.

Who frosted your hair, Duncan Hines?

A: My head hurts.
B: Don't worry. It's not a vital organ.

The Census Bureau told him: You don't count.

They gave him the key to the city . . . dump.

Here's a man who's been called one of the greatest sailors alive today; and he's the one who said it.

Why don't you sing a high note and shatter your head.

He buys his clothes and spark plugs in the same place.

He has an open mind. I can feel the draft from here.

Life is a parade and you're walking behind the elephant.

He took a Greyhound bus, and they made him drive.

He's a loser; he went on jury duty and was found guilty.

Quiet people aren't the only ones who don't say much.

He's so skinny, he walked by a pool room and they chalked him up.

She's got Early American features. She looks like a buffalo.

I'll never forget what you said. But I'll try.

(To an egotist) How do you get your head through doorways?

His career can be summed up in one word: Over.

You have a slow leak under your nose.

You don't get into town much, do you?

I've been his friend for ten years. And there are many reasons for that. Mostly bad luck.

He got a letter from the undertaker signed, "Eventually yours."

He met the mayor of Atlantic City. He gave him the key to a different city.

His ship has just come in; it's the Poseidon.

Congratulations! I heard Harvard wants you to leave your brain . . . to Yale.

You've washed! Where has the week gone!

He donated blood. The family thanked him for saving their dog's life.

If it weren't for Parkay, nobody would talk to him.

He's so exciting, he has a pulse of 1.

The last time I saw a mouth like that, it had a hook in it.

His family is so ugly that in their family album, they only keep the negatives.

He's so skinny, he has to run around in the shower to get wet.

If beauty is only skin deep, you were born inside out.

Is that your nose or are you eating a banana?

Is that your breath or is the circus back in town?

You haven't changed. Why?

A: Nobody likes me.
B: Don't say that! Everyone hasn't met you.

A: Is your voice trained?
B: Yes.
A: Why don't you teach it to roll over and play
      dead.

He started at the bottom and liked it there.

A loser is a guy who plays piano in a marching band.

He reminds me of someone who used to annoy me.

I've seen better shoulders on a popsicle.

I think the stork dropped him on his head.

A: I passed your house last night.
B: Thanks.

(To a skinny guy) A body and a brain to match!

He's so dull, his birthstone is lint.

(After being complimented) I'm sorry I can't return the compliment!

There's no extra cost to anyone but you.

I don't know what makes him so obnoxious. But whatever it is, it works.

He got a bean birthday cake. It tasted pretty awful, but at least it blows out its own candles.

You never looked better. And you never will.

How are things in the intensive care unit?

You'll go into the history books as a bookmark.

He has wavy hair . . . it's waving good-bye.

Boy: What would I have to give you for one little kiss?
Girl: Chloroform

"Do you believe it is possible to communicate with the dead?"
"Yes, I can hear you distinctly."

You have a striking personality. How long has it been on strike?

Of course I'm listening to you; don't you see me yawning?

You talk so much I get hoarse just listening to you.

Things could be worse—you could be here in person.

He has a concrete mind . . . permanently set and all mixed up.

You could make a fortune renting your head out as a balloon.

You have a striking face. How many times have you been struck?

I'm so miserable without you it's almost like you're here.

(To use when you get tongue-tied) "Sorry, I got my tongue in front of my eye tooth, and I couldn't see what I was saying."

So I walked into the art gallery and asked the clerk if she called that horrid picture an old masterpiece. "No, sir," the clerk replied, "That's a mirror."

When I was a little, people used to call me the wonder boy. They used to look at me and wonder.

Our mother used to tell me not to look out of the window, because people would think it's Halloween!

I really watch my weight. It's right out in front where I can see it.

Sometimes I think I understand everything, then I regain consciousness.

When I was young my parents moved to California but I found them.

I had a weird dream last night. I dreamed I was a muffler. Woke up exhausted.

I took an IQ test and the results were negative.

I bought a self-learning record to learn Spanish. I turned it on and went to sleep, and the record got stuck. The next day I could only stutter in Spanish.

I broke my arm trying to fold a bed. . . . It wasn't the kind that folds.

I got a new shadow. I had to get rid of the other one—it wasn't doing what I was doing.

I enjoy being with smart, exciting, and decent people. I also enjoy groups like this!

I have the worst taste in clothes. One day a moth flew into my closet and threw up.

I was so shocked when I was born, I didn't say a word for a year and a half!

My teeth lack calcium. The other day I broke a tooth on Jell-O.

I don't exaggerate. I just remember big!

I'm the kind of guy who gets paper cuts from get-well cards!

I was an unwanted child. When they gave me a rattle, it was still attached to the snake!

It's a good thing I'm schizophrenic. That way, I'm never alone.

I went to the zoo, but the zoo wouldn't accept me!

I'm as confused as a termite in a yo-yo.

I'm sorry I'm late. I locked a coat hanger in my car. It's a good thing I had my keys.

I'm sorry I'm late. I made a U-turn in front of a doughnut shop and 14 policemen gave me a ticket.

I'm sorry I'm late. It takes my wife forever to change a flat.

I've been appointed to the Branson Beautification Committee. My job is to stay out of sight.

I was so fat as a kid, I could only play seek.

I had to stop playing frisbee. It was ruining my teeth.

My teeth were so crooked, I could eat corn on the cob through a tennis racket.

My life has been full of trials, but so far, no convictions!

As a kid I had a lot of charisma, but it's cleared up.

"I just bought a new hearing aid."
"What kind is it?"
"About 4:30."

I'm getting so absentminded that sometimes in the middle of a sentence I . . .

My mind not only wanders, sometimes it leaves completely.

Hey, I don't go down and mess with you when you're working at McDonalds! And I know it must get hot in that clown suit.

He's all right in his place, but they haven't dug it yet!

Do people have to pay you to be that good? No? You mean you're good for nothing?

You look good today. What did you do? Wash?

20

Shopping, Clothing, and Gifts

People have given me a hard time about my wardrobe from time to time. Yes, I am aware that I don't buy Armani. In fact, the average retail value of my wardrobe at any given time is around $56 dollars—and that's including my turquoise jewelry. I don't remember the last time I purchased a clothing item for myself. I think I bought my "We Be Jammin'" t-shirt in 2002; but beyond that, I haven't made many investments in my wardrobe. I figure that, whatever I wear, it couldn't be worse than the white, diamond-studded, spandex jumpsuits we used to wear in the '70s. When you get to that point, anything is an improvement.

The younger generation, however, doesn't remember the white jumpsuits and can only compare my wardrobe to current standards. One day, when my daughter Sarah was in 5th grade, she forgot her lunch at home; so I got in my car and drove down to her elementary school, dressed in one of my routine outfits. I didn't think I looked too bad. I dropped off the lunch and headed back to the house. After I left, one of the kids started making fun of me, saying, "Sarah, look at what your Dad is wearing!" Sarah didn't say much, as she was the new kid in school. She just sat in her seat, sad and quiet. Then, unexpectedly, one of Sarah's classmates started bawling. The teacher was a little alarmed and asked, "What's wrong?" Through her tears, the little girl sobbed, "They're making fun of Sarah's dad!" At least one good thing came from that experience: I found out that I needed a wardrobe update. Still working on that.

Jokes

Shopping tip: You can get shoes for 85 cents at the bowling alley.

Oh, a gift idea. There is a new cologne out for men, that drives women wild. Smells like Wal-Mart!

The other day I went to the Army store to look for some camouflage pants. Couldn't see any.

Dad has always been known for his unique fashion sense. It's not that he doesn't know how to dress, but he just prefers his eclectic ensembles. In 2006, I spent a summer away from home in Nauvoo, Illinois as a performing missionary for the LDS Church. Mom and Dad made the trek to the Midwest to see me perform. Before they arrived, I said to my friends, "Watch, when my Dad gets here, he'll be wearing a black Snap-On hat, his light blue tapered jeans, his Nike zip-up shoes, and either his orange M&M shirt or his Cayman Islands tie-dye shirt." I was right, and that day Dad selected tie-dye. All of my friends thought it was hilarious that I could predict from head to toe what Dad would be wearing.

—*Michelle, Wayne's daughter*

They say that a diamond is forever. The payments are even longer.

First Kid: Thanks very much for the gift you gave me for my birthday.
Second Kid: It was nothing.
First Kid: That's what I thought, but Mom said I had to thank you, anyway!

My wife buys everything that's marked down. Yesterday she came home with an escalator!

What do you call an artificial stone? A shamrock.

Where does a one-armed man shop? At a second-hand store.

Never buy Q-Tips at the nearly new shop.

I thought you'd like to know my shirt size is 15 ½, my shoes size is 9 ½, and if you're considering a cash gift I take an extra large.

Olive Osmond

Wayne used to wear suspenders with his pants and pull them up so tight we would say he had the waist near his armpits—but he must have felt more secure with them "tight" because that's the way he always wore them. He loved wearing a little cowboy hat, too. One day he came from the kitchen into the dining room doing a little shuffle with one foot. Then he said, "Not many kids can do that." (We still use that saying.)

. . . . Olive Osmond . .

Wayne was always very neat and meticulous with everything he did. His clothes were always hung up neatly when he took them off (and he immediately changed his clothes when he came home from school or church without being asked). His wardrobe closet was always in order. He took such good care of his toys and other belongings, they were almost like new from one Christmas to the next.

The perfect gift for the person who has everything is a burglar alarm.

"Whenever I'm down in the dumps I get new clothes."
"I wondered where you got your clothes."

I have such bad luck. I bought an electric blanket and it's solar powered.

A fellow who was all out of birthday gift ideas for his mother-in-law wound up buying her a large plot in an expensive cemetery. For her next birthday, he bought nothing. When she complained vociferously about his thoughtlessness he said, "Well, you didn't use the gift I gave you last year."

I found a worm in my earth shoes.

I bought my son an indestructible toy. Yesterday he left it in the driveway. It broke my car.

Corduroy pillows: They're making headlines!

I bought my kid an educational toy to help him make it through life. No matter how you put it together, it's wrong.

He's a man of rare gifts. Nobody ever got one from him.

She said she wanted to see the world, so he bought her a map.

He's the kind of cheap guy who'd buy himself a wind-up pacemaker.

He'd give you the sleeves off his vest.

The post office is very careful nowadays. When they get a package marked "Fragile," they throw it underhand.

When companies ship styrofoam, what do they pack it in?

You can't have everything. Where would you put it?

My dad was always my hero. He was so fun to be around and knew how to make everything. One of my favorite projects was when we stained and branded a leather belt. It took several days to make (and to a six-year-old kid, that's forever), but it was worth the time! I wore it everywhere I went. It even had a nice gold, shiny buckle just like the buckles that Dad wore on stage. Now that I am a few years older and a few pounds heavier, the belt is too small for me to wear; but my six-year-old boy Paul loves wearing it and hearing the story of how his daddy and his grandpa made that belt together.

—*Steve, Wayne's son*

Dad has great fashion sense—when it comes to women's clothing. When he buys clothes for Mom, you can count on them being classy and cute. But when it comes to his own clothes, he couldn't care less.

A few years ago, my dad came to meet us at Greg's soccer game in what could easily be described as the "clashiest" combination I've ever seen. He wore his car-mechanic-greasy jogging pants that were two inches too short; black, textured dress socks; worn-out black loafers with gold buckles; a white linen shirt patterned with fluorescent pink and orange flowers; a brown tweed jacket; and an Army cap. I kid you not, this outfit could not have been more mismatched if he tried.

The great thing about Dad, though, is he simply doesn't care. No apologies, no insecurities. As long as he's warm and comfortable, he's just happy to be there.

—*Amy, Wayne's daughter*

I went to the store the other day and asked the guy if I could see something cheap in a suit. He said, "Look in the mirror."

21

Sports and Exercise

As an entertainer, I have devoted my life to music. I estimate that I have spent approximately seven hours a day since the time I was six years old singing and learning to play thirteen instruments. This left little time for sports. Even though I was never on sports teams in high school (I was taking correspondence classes!), I always found a place in my life for exercise.

I enjoyed sports as much as the next kid. Kickball, baseball, and running were my personal favorites. I was in the 5th grade when I became the champion marble player at Lincoln Elementary School. I had learned how to shoot marbles on asphalt and practiced a lot. When I went to play the champions of the other schools in the district, I got slaughtered because they played on dirt instead of asphalt. It was disappointing.

In the 7th grade I wanted to be healthy so I started doing the Canadian Air Force Exercise Regimen. This regimen required me to run a precise distance every day and do overall strength training, such as push-ups and sit-ups. I also read all of Adele Davis's health books and made myself blender drinks with brewer's yeast and protein powder. I eventually worked up to the top level of the exercise regimen.

In the 8th grade, I had a gym teacher that didn't like the Osmonds. He was upset that I missed school to perform and was literally out to get me. One time, he gave the class a fitness test one at a time and saved me for last. When it was my turn he said to me in front of the class, "You haven't been at school to work on your push-ups and sit-ups. You are not going to make it through this test, and you are not going to pass my class." Then he made everyone stand around while I did my test so they could all laugh at me.

Well, this gym teacher didn't know that I was doing the Canadian exercise regimen. That combined with pure embarrassment made me determined to pass his test, pass the class, and never have to see him again. The other boys in the class could do about 40 push-ups; my teacher stopped me when I got to 70. The other guys in gym class did about 30 sit-ups; he made me stop after 70. The other boys did about 10 pull-ups each; and he

---

Dad taught Steve and me how to fly fish. We used to practice at home in the yard. One time he took us up Provo Canyon to the Provo River. Every time I tried to cast the fishing rod out into the river, it would get caught in the brush behind me. One time, as I tried to cast the fishing rod out, I heard a yelp. Dad had the misfortune of standing behind me, and the hook had gotten caught in the neck of his coat. He never could get the hook out from under the neck of the coat, but he didn't let that bother him. He wore it proudly for years.

—Greg, Wayne's son

made me quit after 30 pull-ups. He got really mad when I started doing one-armed pull-ups, so he made me stop after three or four. In the timed sprint, I was the fastest runner in the class. He never looked at me again for the rest of the year. Thank goodness.

Jokes about sports are great, as long as you don't get too technical. The following jokes are generic enough for people of all ages and levels of expertise to enjoy.

Jokes

Whenever you go golfing, make sure you wear two pair of pants in case you get a hole in one.

If you're going to try cross-country skiing, start with a small country.

When Jay was young, he had a "rocket arm." He could throw the football like you can't believe. So, he wanted to join a team. The coach gave him the football and said, "Can you pass this?" Jay said, "Heck, I can't even swallow it!"

The kid struck out so many times in Little League that his father traded him!

If swimming is good for your shape, then why do the whales look the way they do?

He was a colorful fighter—black and blue and bloody.

One boxer who got knocked out a lot made a fortune. He sold advertising space on the bottoms of his shoes.

I'll never forget this one girl I met. I got such a lump in my throat. She was a karate champ!

I jog everywhere for my health, but I never find it!

I woke up this morning with a real desire to exercise. So I stayed in bed till the desire went away!

Fishing is a sport with a worm at one end and a dummy at the other!

Fishing is a jerk on one end of the line waiting for a jerk on the other!

One day, Dad took Greg and me into the wilderness to learn how to camp and use a compass. The truth of the matter was that he had never done it before, but to us he was a regular mountain man. Our first task when we arrived at our campsite was to use a compass to navigate through the woods and then arrive back to camp safely. With our dad leading us, we navigated through the woods and slowly watched the confidence on his face being replaced with confusion. I knew then that we were lost.

A bad storm was now approaching, and he was starting to get nervous. We knelt down and prayed for Heavenly Father to guide us and direct us back to our camp. We got up and started walking; and in just a few minutes we found ourselves back at our camp! Dad may not have been able to master a traditional compass, but he taught me a much more important lesson—when you are in a difficult situation, the person you turn to is God. (Oh, we ended up that night not in a tent but in a nearby hotel watching TV and ordering pizza. Dad always knew how to have fun. Thanks, Dad!)

—Steve, Wayne's son

Pro linemen are so big, it only takes three of them to make a dozen!

I like to bet on jockeys with bad breath. The horses win just trying to get away from them!

My horse was so slow, it ran faster when it became glue!

My horse said to his jockey, "Why are you hitting me? There's nobody behind us!"

I'm a little wary of people who use my pool. Last year, when I filled it, I put in ten thousand gallons. Later in the year I emptied it and took out eleven thousand!

The human race has got to be the slowest and most boring sporting event ever started.

Never fall in love with a tennis player. To them love means nothing.

Why do we sing "Take Me Out to the Ball Game" when we are already there?

The reason it's called "golf" is because all the other four-letter words were taken.

I don't jog. I don't play tennis. I exercise by visiting friends in the hospital that jog and play tennis.

"I hear your son's on the high school football team," said the neighbor. "What position does he play?" "I'm not sure," said the parent. "I think he's a drawback."

Jay tried out for football but they already had one.

I wondered why the baseball was getting bigger. Then it hit me.

22

Traveling

I'm not offended if people call me forgetable, but I know it's bad when my own flesh and blood can't remember me. When I was 21 years old, we were on the road one day and made a routine pit stop at a gas station. We all got off the bus to get a snack, and I had to use the restroom. Well, let's just say that I was detained a little longer than I had anticipated. When I got back to the bus, there was no bus. At first I thought it was a joke, because it was like my brothers—and especially like my sister—to pull a prank like this. But I quickly realized that it was no joke; they had really driven off without me. I had no way to contact them, so all I could do was wait and hope that they would come back to get me. As it turned out, they didn't realize I was missing until they had driven fifty miles. That made me feel pretty special. I guess I should just be grateful that they did eventually turn around to get me.

This traveling mishap was just one of many. When we all moved to Branson, our agent stressed how important it was for us to go to bus conventions and do shows to build our bus base. One particular time, we (the band, dancers, singers, crew, and brothers) were scheduled to fly in two Merlin airplanes to perform at a convention. The weather was horrible and the pilot warned us not to go, but the woman in charge was adamant.

During the flight, the pilot tried to dodge the bad areas of the storm; but one time he didn't have any choice but to go through eight thunderheads. The whole plane rolled—and it felt like it was coming apart. We became increasingly nervous as bags dropped from the overhead compartments and people who didn't wear seatbelts were suspended in the air. At the height of the storm, an open ice chest spewed its contents into the cabin. I had watched the ice chest come apart, but everyone else thought the ice was coming from outside the plane. The woman in charge screamed, "We're gonna die!" and others were praying. I personally thought it was a fun ride! But I will admit that I hoped the wings of the plane wouldn't come off.

Jokes

"How often do those big jets crash?"
"Once, I imagine!"

I've been staying in this really posh hotel. The pillows are so big and fluffy, I can hardly close my suitcase.

If you look like the picture in your passport, you probably need the trip!

A friend of mine sent me a postcard with a satellite photo of the entire planet on it. On the back he wrote, "Wish you were here."

Unforgetable newspaper advertisement: Wanted—Man to understudy human cannonball. Must be willing to travel!

I'm suffering from bus lag.

About an hour after the flight started, the pilot announced, "Ladies and gentlemen, I'm afraid we'll have to slow down because of the loss of our number-one engine. A few minutes later, the second engine went out and a similar announcement was made. The plane would have to slow down more. Then the third engine went out. A passenger turned to the man next to him and said, "If that last one goes, we'll be up here all night!"

Airlines are mean. They send your luggage to places you can't afford to go!

There was a no-frills airline. Twenty minutes before the flight, the passengers got together to elect a pilot!

We were going to fly this no-frills airline, but they pulled the steps away and the plane fell over!

You can become a little upset when you go to the airline counter to complain about lost luggage and the ticket agent is wearing your clothes!

On a recent flight, three engines went out. Wearing a parachute, the pilot appeared in front of the passengers and announced, "We've got a lot of problems, but don't worry—I'm going for help!"

The in-flight movie was so bad the passengers walked out!

Then there's Gypsy Airlines. It has the lowest fares in the country, but when you land your wallet will be gone!

She said she wanted to see the world—so he bought her a map.

I'm very lucky. I've been to Europe almost as often as my luggage!

My wake-up call was missed by a day and a half.

One woman told another, "Last year we took a trip around the world. This year we're going someplace else!"

My wife must be descended from Noah. When we travel, she takes two of everything! ·

I took a look at my passport picture and decided I looked too sick to travel!

Never stay in a hotel with "vacant" painted on the side.

So what's the speed of dark?

Solitude . . . a great place to visit, but a bad place to stay.

My First Jet Ride
(Wayne's High School English Paper)

My first jet ride took place in 1961 between Salt Lake City, Utah, and San Francisco, California.

The S.P.E.B.S.Q.S.A (Society for the Preservation and Encouragement of Barbershop Quartet Singing in America) had invited my brothers and me to perform for their national convention. We were honored, excited and delighted until we found out we were going to fly. Then fear hit us, especially me.

For almost a week I couldn't eat or sleep. I didn't even listen to what the teacher said in school. I was literally dreading that "count down" of days.

Finally the day arrived. We closed the lid on our suitcase, drove to Salt Lake, kissed our mother good-bye and climbed aboard. (I was the last one and kept looking back and waving, wishing I could find some way to get out of there.)

The shortest distance between two points is closed for construction.

Never eat in a restaurant where you see a cockroach bench pressing a burrito.

This hotel room is so small I put the key in the door and broke the window.

A ship sailing from Hong Kong with a cargo of yo-yos collided with another ship and sank 164 times.

I know a guy who was on a tour of Europe. He got into a street fight in Venice and nearly drowned.

We found our seats and the stewardess strapped us in. Then she began demonstrating what we should do if we needed oxygen or got sick. That didn't calm me down one bit.

The engines roared, the seats vibrated, I shut my eyes and said a prayer. Father patted me on the shoulder and I felt a little better. Then, suddenly we really took off. The ground was literally whizzing by. I realized we were leaving good old "terra firma" —but fast.

The stewardess brought us a snack, some games, some soda pop. Hmmm! This wasn't so bad after all.

We were in San Francisco in nothing flat and I could hardly wait to go home so I could ride on another jet. I've loved flying ever since; in fact, I will soon have my private pilot's license.

That airline is so bad, the oxygen masks were already hanging down when we got on.

A: Have a rough trip?

B: No thanks, just had one.

I took one of those cheap flights on an airline. When I finished eating, I had to do the dishes.

Sign on restaurant door: If you want home-cooked meals, eat at home.

My airplane flight was so rough that the stewardesses poured the food directly into the sick sacks!

Travel broadens a person. You look like you've been all over the world.

23

Seasons and Weather

Every year, I spend most of the winter wondering why I live in Utah. I inherited my father's bad circulation, and I'm always cold! Even when I was a young kid, I couldn't handle the cold weather. When I walked home from school, I had to stop at my grandmother's house on the way to warm my cold and aching arms under the running hot water. I love being warm! It's not uncommon to see me on a Caribbean cruise with my winter coat on.

In theory, I'm an outdoorsy guy. But only when the weather is good. When my sons were young, I wanted them to experience fishing. So, I took them up to Strawberry Lake in Northern Utah. We got to our destination, only to be met with bitter wind, torrential rains, and intimidating thunder and lightning. I was certainly not going outside in that weather! So instead, we sat in the car, talked, and watched a tree get blown to bits by a bolt of lightning. After a while, we decided to bag the fishing trip and go to the movies.

The next year, I decided to take my boys on another fishing trip. This time I was determined to actually fish. But, no. We experienced the exact same bout of wind, rain, and lightning—and again opted for the movies. My boys may not be the best fishermen on earth, but they are very good movie critics!

Weather jokes have always been staples, but they've lost a little of their luster in recent years. Perhaps we are not as dependent on the weather; or perhaps we don't get outside enough to notice. Whatever the reason, unless you live in Minnesota or Arizona on a record-setting day, people are not as likely to view weather as an important enough topic to be worthy of a joke.

Weather jokes can still be good, however, when paired with another human interest element. One of my favorite jokes to tell on stage is, "It was so cold today, I saw a politician with his hands in his own pockets." See? It worked—greediness and weather all wrapped up in a perfect punchline.

Jokes

It was so cold you had to part your hair with an ax.

It was so hot the other day I saw a dog chasing a cat and they were walking.

How are a Texas tornado and a Tennessee divorce the same? Somebody's gonna lose a trailer.

What do you get when you cross a snowman with a vampire? Frostbite.

It's going to be a rough winter. I just saw a squirrel steal four acorns and a can of Sterno!

Last week the beach was really crowded. I had to dive in six times before I hit water!

Our local TV weatherman was fired. He couldn't even predict yesterday's weather!

I try to clean up the air—I inhale.

Dew is a big problem on my lawn. Every morning ten dogs "dew" on it!

Smog is bad for people like me. I'm a chain breather.

The smog is real bad. This morning I saw a robin breathing through a worm.

I never believed I'd see the day when indirect lighting meant the sun.

The other day they filled the Goodyear blimp with air, and it died!

It was raining so hard I got seasick walking home!

Feb. 11, 1985

Dear Mother and Father,

Well, it surely is good to be back in Provo; even if it is the coldest place in the world! The other night, at a weather station called "Peter Sink," they measured a 69.9 below zero! It was colder here than in Alaska! We've been flying in the "Westwind" jet lately. I have, of course, spent most of the time in the cockpit. What a way to travel! We took off from Salt Lake the other day because Provo's runways hadn't been cleared so they couldn't land. We were going to Florida to do some shows. When you go from west to east, you can take advantage of the "jet stream"; so, we had a registered ground speed of 565 mph! It's so much nicer than flying commercially.

Well, I surely will be glad to see you when we come over in April!

Love you guys,

Wayne

It was so windy the other day, I saw a Siamese twin looking for the other one!

He's so tall, six months a year he goes around with snow on his head!

You know it's real wintry when you comb your hair outside and it breaks!

It was so cold the other night, our snowman was trying to get into the house!

It was so cold yesterday, men were wearing their toupees upside down!

The best device for clearing the driveway of snow is a kid who wants to use the car.

The reason lightning doesn't strike twice in the same place is the same place usually isn't there the second time.

Never search for an albino in a blizzard.

If lightning strikes, make sure you're walking next to a tall person.

My dad is a wimp when it comes to cold temperatures. I remember looking at the sidelines for Dad during my last football game of the season in high school. I could see Mom, my grandpa and grandma, and a large pile of blankets. I found out after the game that the pile of blankets was actually my dad. I teased Dad that he stole my 70-year-old grandma's blanket to stay warm. He never denied it!

—Steve, Wayne's son

(When it's hot) After the meeting, we're all going to get together and toast marshmallows on the air conditioner.

It was raining cats and dogs, and I almost stepped in a "Poodle."

Her hair was blowing in the wind; and she was too proud to run after it.

It was so windy that Clint Eastwood's face blew into a different expression.

A day without sunshine is like night.

24

Wife and Family

In January 1973, my parents purchased the Riviera Apartments in Provo, Utah, right across from Brigham Young University. We lived in the apartments, along with thousands of college students. Though our performing schedule precluded us from attending college, my mother and father wanted us to experience the social aspect of college life. In other words, I think they wanted me to find a wife and give them some grandkids.

I wanted nothing more than to find a soulmate. I had dated a lot since the time I was sixteen, but I hadn't found that special connection I was looking for. On a Sunday evening, when I was twenty-two years old, I asked Heavenly Father if I could meet someone that could become special to me.

The next Sunday, I went to church and sat with a girl I was casually dating at the time. The meeting started and the conductor announced the program agenda, including a vocal solo by Kathlyn White. When it came time for the musical number, I suddenly saw the most beautiful woman I had ever seen. She had gorgeous long dark hair, beautiful lips, and big green eyes. It was love at first sight! But not only was she gorgeous, she also sang like an angel. I saw a beautiful aura form around her and a voice whispered, "There she is."

I could hardly wait for the meeting to finish. I excused myself from my date and went immediately to the front of the church where Kathlyn was being surrounded by admiring men. I felt a pang of guilt for being rude to my date, but when I saw my future wife all of the bells and whistles went off, and I could not control myself. I mustered up the courage to introduce myself and, a week later, gathered up my courage again to ask her on a date. To my surprise, she agreed; and eleven months later we were married in the Salt Lake Temple for eternity.

I wanted everything to be perfect for our wedding day, but it didn't start out too well. I was nervous and had forgotten our marriage license and had to drive back home in the worst snowstorm of the year to get it. I was so late, Kathy's mother wondered if I had left her at the altar. Kathy assured her mother that I would come through, and I eventually made it—over an hour late.

The comedy of errors continued. At the wedding luncheon, Donny and Marie handcuffed Kathy and me together, which I could handle because it was really kind of cute. But after our reception, I got a little bit irritated. Donny had snuck out of the reception early and had completely destroyed my car. Cardboard was stuffed in every nook and cranny so tightly that we couldn't get in to drive away. Whipped cream was smeared all over the outside *and inside* of the car. I can't even imagine how many cans he used. The steering wheel was so slippery, driving was hazardous. Cans were tied to the car and were dragging along with us. My brothers must have been up all night drinking soda to produce that many empty cans. Now it's pretty funny, and I can appreciate all of Donny's hard work to make our wedding reception memorable. But at the time, I remember worrying what Kathy would think about my crazy family.

Since that time I have never had a moment of doubt or regret about marrying my Kathy. She is truly my soulmate, and I am looking forward to spending the rest of eternity with her.

Jokes

When Jay was a baby his parents baby-proofed the house, but he still got in.

"If we get engaged would you give me a ring?"
"Sure, what's your number?"

A woman's word is never done.

Olive Osmond

My father (Thomas M. Davis) had nicknames for all my kids. He called them their "pet names." He chose "Wonky Donkey" for Wayne and it sounded cute. Wayne seemed to enjoy it so we used it often - lovingly.

One day, a fellow from the feed store delivered some grain for our cow and as he walked to the house to bring me the bill, he turned to Wayne and said, "What's your name, young man?"

"Wonky Donkey" was the reply. The look on the man's face told me maybe we'd better start calling him Wayne.

My wife said, "You remind me of the sea."
"Is that because I'm so wild and romantic?"
"No, it's because you make me sick."

I knew we were going to have problems in the marriage when she wanted to be in all the wedding pictures.

The policeman said, "Did you know that you left your wife at the gas station?"
"What a relief! I thought I had gone deaf."

Do you know my wife? She's got a face like a million dollars—green and wrinkled!

On our honeymoon, my wife and I were lying on the beach. I was lying to her and she was lying to me.

My wife and I bought a waterbed when we first got married. We've been drifting apart ever since.

My wife didn't want to get married because the hours were too long.

The one thing that we had in common was the kids. She didn't want them and neither did I.

My wife's a treasure—she's worth her weight in plastic.

Did you hear about the wife who had plastic surgery? Her husband cut up her credit cards.

I love being married. It's so great to find that one special person you want to annoy for the rest of your life.

I married my wife for her looks—but not the ones she's been giving me lately!

My mother said I was a procrastinator. I said, "Oh yeah? You just wait."

The way to a woman's heart is through a Porsche.

Did you hear that the invisible man married the invisible woman? Their kids weren't much to look at, either.

Why can't a woman ask her brother for help? Because he can't be a brother and assist her too.

So I bought my wife a mood ring. When she's in a good mood it turns green. When she's in a bad mood I get a red mark on my forehead.

Do you know why my wife washes in Tide? 'Cause it's too cold out-tide.

Why do women quit having children at 36? Because 36 is enough!

Wife: Did you ever notice the Wymans next door? How loving they are? How he always puts his arms around her and kisses her when he comes home? Why don't you do that?
Husband: If I knew her better, I would.

A woman comes home shouting, "Honey, pack your bags! I won the lottery!" The husband exclaims, "Wow! That's great! Should I pack for the ocean, for the mountains, or what?" And she says, "I don't care. Just get the heck out."

A: Did you know that the shortest sentence in the English language is, "I am"?
B: Really? What's the longest sentence?
A: "I do."

When I was a kid, we were so poor that when my little brother broke his arm we had to take him out to the airport for x-rays.

School days are the happiest of your life, but only if your children are old enough to attend!

Adam and Eve had a great marriage. Adam couldn't bring up his mother's cooking, and Eve couldn't talk about the man she was supposed to marry!

I think our builder made a mistake. I even said that to my wife this morning when I was walking downstairs to the attic.

Nurse: Sir, you've just become the father of twins.
Man: Don't tell my wife. I want to surprise her.

A bachelor is a man who doesn't have anybody to share the trouble he'd have if he was married.

A bachelor is a man who's crazy to get married, and he knows it.

Bachelors know more about women than married men do, which could explain why they're still single.

"My nurse used to drop me a lot."
"What did your mother do?"
"She got me a shorter nurse!"

"My sister is going to have a baby."
"Did you call her up?"
"I don't have to. She knows about it!"

The day my kid was born, he cried like a baby!

When she went to a beauty parlor, she had to use the emergency entrance! And when she finally came in, the staff would start to hum "The Impossible Dream."

My wife gives our leftovers to our cat. The vet says that the cat only has four lives left!

She's a terrible cook. This afternoon she burned her shopping list.

I miss my wife's cooking—every chance I get!

I came home the other night. My wife was in tears because the dog had eaten one of her chicken pot pies. I said, "Stop crying. I'll buy you another dog."

She gives me a lot of health food, so I always have natural gas!

"What did your daughter do last summer?"
"Her hair and her nails!"

A daughter is a young lady who always marries a man of much lower mental capacity than she does and yet manages to have utterly brilliant children.

"What is your daughter taking in college?"
"Everything I've got!"

"Son, this is going to hurt me more than it hurts you."
"Well, make sure you go easy on yourself!"

"Did I ever tell you about my kid?"
"No, and I appreciate it!"

I figured out why they call our language the "mother tongue." Father never gets a chance to use it!

My wife never throws anything out. The other night she made hamburgers. I couldn't eat mine, so she used it to clean the sink!

We just celebrated our tin anniversary—fifteen years of eating out of cans.

Girls are dynamite. If you don't believe that, try dropping one.

She's like a photograph of her father and a phonograph of her mother!

She knew her oats. That's what they fed her!

Never marry a girl who can open envelopes with her breath!

She was a cover girl. When a guy met her, he ran for cover!

Home is where you wait until your son brings home the car!

The cab arrived at the hotel. Getting out, the new bride asked her husband, "What can we do to hide the fact that we've just been married?" The groom said, "You carry the luggage!"

He's a model husband, but not a working model!

We share household chores. I dry the dishes. My wife sweeps them up!

A man worked out his budget and told his wife, "One of us will have to go!"

I just bought my wife a one million dollar life insurance policy. Now every time I leave the house, she says, "Have a good day, and take chances!"

An insurance agent told a newlywed man, "Now that you're married, you should take out some insurance." The man said, "Nah, I don't think my wife will be dangerous!"

Jenny watched her mother put cream on her face and asked, "What's that cream for?" The mother said, "It's facial cream to make me look gorgeous." A few minutes later, the mother removed the cream. Jenny stared and then said, "I knew it wouldn't work."

The new baby was bawling in his crib as his five-year-old brother stood by. The five-year-old asked his mother as she started to attend the infant, "Where'd we get him?"

The mother said, "He came from heaven." The baby screamed again and the five-year-old said, "I can see why they threw him out!"

I told my wife that a husband is like a fine wine—he gets better with age. The next day she locked me in the cellar.

My wife and I never go to bed mad. We stay up until the problem is resolved. Last year we didn't get to sleep until March!

My wife and I have a perfect understanding. I don't try to run her life and I don't try to run mine!

"Will you love me when I'm old and bald?"
"It's tough enough now, when you're young and hairy!"

My uncle believes that marriage and a career don't mix, so when he got married he stopped working!

Armed by a pep talk from someone he'd met at a bar, a man went home and bellowed to his wife, "From now on, I'm the king of this castle. My word is law. When I want to eat, you run in and cook. When I want my bath, you start the water. We can start right now. Lay out my tuxedo because I'm going out—alone! And do you know who's going to tie my black tie?" His wife said softly, "The undertaker!"

Most wives lead double lives—their husbands' and their own.

My wife lets me wear the pants in the family—right under my apron!

My wife never lies about her age. She just tells people she's as old as I am. Then she lies about my age!

I can make my wife do anything she wants to do.

I'm growing old by myself. My wife hasn't had a birthday in ten years!

She doesn't show her age, but if you look under her makeup it's there.

She was named after Betsy Ross, but not long after!

"Dad, where are the Himalayas?"
"Ask your mother. She puts everything away!"

A teenage girl said to her mother, "Don't yell at me. I'm not your husband!"

Parents spend the first few years of a child's life trying to get him to talk. They spend the rest trying to get the kid to shut up!

The babysitter didn't voice an objection because the parents were so late, saying, "Don't apologize. I wouldn't be in a hurry to come home, either!"

There's only one way to handle a woman, but nobody knows which way that is!

He's not choosy. He likes her for what she is—rich!

He was so poor, his parents used to buy bread in the day-old bakery. Until he was sixteen, he thought whole wheat was green!

I knew a guy who was so poor he got married just for the rice!

The bride said, "My little plum."
The groom said, "My little peach."
The minister said, "I now pronounce you fruit salad!"

My family used to hang around a lot, especially from trees!

He married a girl who could take a joke—him!

My wife wanted beautiful roses like those next door, so I waited until it got dark.

"Who's that ugly man over there?"
"My brother."
"Really? There's a striking family resemblance!"

Families are like fudge—mostly sweet with a few nuts.

It's not too bad when you have twin babies. When one cries, you can't hear the other one!

He didn't go to his own wedding. Nobody invited him!

Don't leave me," the wife sobbed to her dying husband. "Don't go. I can't be without you. Don't leave me." The dying husband said, "Okay, come with me!"

"That's a nice coat. Did your husband change jobs?"
"No, I changed husbands!"

A wife had her face lifted, her nose straightened out, her legs shaped, her bosom curved, yet she still turned to her husband and said, "You're not the same man I married!"

My wife complained about not being wanted, so I went to the post office and put up her picture!

My wife doesn't clean much. In the living room we have a copy of "Good Housekeeping" covered with 3 inches of dust.

My wife should go into earthquake work. She can find a fault quicker than anybody.

My wife dislocated her jaw and couldn't speak. I called the doctor immediately and told him to come by as soon as he came back from his vacation.

If my wife dies, I'm going to marry her sister so I don't have to break in another mother-in-law.

The last fight was my fault. My wife asked, "What's on the TV?" I said, "Dust!"

My wife's a terrible cleaner. She keeps clogging up the dishwasher with paper plates!

At times I help my wife in the kitchen. I help put out the fire!

I shouldn't have bought her a microwave oven. Now I have to eat her food fifteen minutes sooner!

My wife doesn't need to call us when dinner is ready. We can tell because the smoke alarm goes off!

In my house, when you ask, "Guess who's coming to dinner?" The answer is usually "the paramedics!"

She feeds him so much fish he's growing gills.

We have the only garbage disposal with ulcers!

My wife throws away the leftovers, but I want her to throw away the originals!

A father told his son, "Hard work never killed anybody." The son answered, "I'm looking for something dangerous!"

An old axiom: Do not argue with your wife while she is packing your parachute.

Be nice to your kids. They'll choose your nursing home.

Behind every successful man is a surprised mother-in-law.

Mrs. Murphy's Law: If anything can go wrong, it will go wrong when he's out of town.

How does a spoiled rich girl change a lightbulb? She says, "Daddy, I want a new apartment."

I wanted to come up with something I could hang on the wall as a token to remember all of our years together; but, how do you frame an ulcer?

Merrill told mother he was running away. She said, "On your mark . . ."

Before I was married I tried one of those online dating services. I said I liked water sports and formal wear. I got matched up with a penguin.

Saturday, Aug. 6, 1966

Huntsville, Utah

Dear Diary,

Today we got up, got dressed in yellow shirts, black pants and black shoes. We went to the park at 38th and Jackson in Ogden to have the family reunion. Uncle Ralph was in charge this year so he and his family were already there. Soon all of the families were there. We played a lot of baseball and then ate yogurt, chicken, fruit salad, root beer and all of the other things you usually have at reunions.

We played a lot of games, sang songs and then Jimmy sang "Red Roses for a Blue Lady" with us as backgrounds and then we sang "O Here's a Song." Later went back to Huntsville, practiced our instruments. Mother and I talked about airplanes, we practiced instruments AND (I made such a big "and" just now because the wind sucked the door closed and it scared me!) that evening we went to bed.

My grandmother lived to be 93 and never needed glasses. She drank straight from the bottle.

"Dad, will you take me to the zoo?"
"Son, I've told you fifty times, if the zoo wants you, they'll come and get you."

My parents were in the iron and steel business. My mother would iron and my dad would steal.

A friend of mine confused her Valium with her birth control pills. She had 14 kids, but she doesn't really care.

Dad was cheap. He read in the paper that it takes 10 dollars a year to support a kid in India—so that's where he sent us.

The reason grandchildren and grandparents get along so well is that they have a common enemy.

My dad was a wonderful example of humility to me growing up. I always knew that he was very talented, but he never looked at himself as a star or famous. He has never been proud. One time, I remember that he was given a volunteer assignment at church. I thought that it must be a very important job because he was such an amazing guy. The next Sunday, he began his job as the usher, walking around greeting people in the congregation and handing out hymn books. I thought to myself, "There's no way I would ever accept the job to handout hymn books." I asked Dad why he accepted such a menial job that anyone could do. His answer: "It doesn't matter what the job is. As long as you are serving others you are serving the Savior."

—*Steve, Wayne's son*

My kid's mean. He tapes worms to the sidewalk and watches the birds get hernias.

Marriage is nature's way of keeping people from fighting with strangers.

You know how big our Osmond family is? It's so big that I have a hard time remembering all the names of the children of my brothers and sister. So, I came up with a great solution. It's easy. I just call all the girls Denise. And all the boys I call Denephew.

| Mr. Green: | My wife is very poetic. She gets up at sunrise and says, "Lo, the morn!" |
| Mr. Gray: | What?! You lucky man. My wife gets up and says, "Mow the lawn!" |

The other day I discovered that I descended from royalty. King Kong.

You have to stay in shape. My grandmother started walking five miles a day when she was 60. She's 97 today and we don't know where the heck she is.

I looked up my wife's family tree the other day, and half of them are still living in it.

I looked up my family tree and found out I was the sap.

Shake any family tree and a few nuts will fall.

His ancestor was a deck chair on the Mayflower.

She's always late. Her ancestors arrived on the June-flower.

My grandmother came across the plains in a covered wagon. If you'd have seen her face, you'd know why they covered it.

I think her gene pool is more of a puddle.

You! Out of the gene pool now!

The gene pool could use a little chlorine.

The problem with the gene pool is that there's no life-guard.

He looks like the funny papers after the kids read it.

Definition of "Boss": The thing Mother allows Father to think that he is.

I married Miss Right. I just didn't know her first name was Always.

I haven't spoken to my wife in 18 months—I don't like to interrupt her.

Baby philosophy: If it stinks, change it.

The best way to keep kids at home is to make the home a pleasant atmosphere and let the air out of their tires.

He: Want to get married? It'd be easy, my dad's a minister.
She: We could give it a try; my dad's a lawyer.

My dad is the best grandpa in the whole world. When we tell the kids that Grandpa Osmond is coming to visit, my little girl Aili gets so excited that she will see "Silly Grandpa." Aili then tells me of all the places that she and her grandpa will be going: "the candy store, the ice cream shop, the airplane museum, and then the ice cream shop again."
—*Steve, Wayne's son*

Love letter from Father George to Mother Olive
May 23, 1985. London, England

Dearest Olive,

I am here sitting on pins and needles waiting for your call to let me know about your foot. I'm sure that you will be okay and that we can "hoe to the end of the row." . . . It is our day off tomorrow and I think I will go to Que Gardens or someplace for the day. I guess I'll have to admit it but I think you're super and without you, I just wouldn't want to fight it. What I'm trying to say is that I love you, Jo, and I want you happy. . . .

One thing is bothering me. I worry about you not using your bus pass enough. That is such a good deal, we must take advantage of it. Ha. Ha.

It's 10:00 and you have not called me—darn it. You know how impatient I am. . . . I have not bought any groceries since you left. You should see the fridge.

I have been writing in my journal every day. I have not been correcting the spelling or the punctuation so it makes it a little harder to read.

That's all you get tonight my dear. I hope you are not in any kind of pain unless it's your love for me. Believe me, I know how it feels as I sure love you. Bye for now.

—*Your George*

Acknowledgments

This book wouldn't have happened without the help of many people. I thank my brothers and sister, with whom I have shared an amazing lifetime adventure. I love and appreciate you all. I thank my parents, who believed in and showed unparalleled devotion to their children—I miss you. I thank my daughters Michelle and Amy, for helping me compile the information in this book; and my children Steve, Greg, and Sarah, for adding stories and memories. Thank you to Sourced Media Books for publishing this book and making it the best it can be. And to my wife, Kathy, thank you for being my companion for 35 wonderful years. I can't wait to see what the next 35 will bring!

A Tribute from Kathy

Much has been written about the Osmonds over the past fifty years, but not much has been written about Wayne as an individual. As one of nine children and an introvert by nature, Wayne has preferred to stay in a supporting role. Producer, sound engineer, accountant, and songwriter are some of the other enjoyable hats he has worn to support his brothers and sister. Though he isn't as well-known as some of his siblings, Wayne has etched out his own identity. His audiences know him as "Crazy Wayne," the one who is long winded, tells a lot of jokes and acts silly. Wayne is also known by many other names, including Melvin, Mel, Wonk, Wonkey Donkey, Wings, Squeek, Squeeker, the smartest Osmond, and the dumbest Osmond. I would like to pay tribute to the man who, through all the rollercoasters of his life in show business, has kept his standards, ideals, humility and compassion for others. I would like to add my tribute to the serious side of Melvin Wayne Osmond which audiences may not see but his family knows so well.

When I met Wayne, the first thing that I noticed was how his eyes twinkled. I loved the fact that he was religious and spiritual yet could still enjoy life and have a lot of fun. Wayne had so many talents and interests that I knew I'd be exposed to many new and exciting things whenever I was around him. He was surprised when I accepted an invitation for our first official date, and he was sincerely interested in me. I loved being with him—our communication flowed and he was really easy to talk with. I remember wondering if he really was "for real," because we agreed on everything that we talked about.

At the end of our first date, I thought to myself, "He is the first guy that I have known that I could possibly marry." I brushed off the thought; I was sure that was how everyone felt that went on a date with Wayne. As our love progressed, I was introduced to his family and felt an immediate bond with them, like I had already known them. I also brushed off that thought, because I knew that was how everyone that met the Osmonds felt about them. They were warm, friendly, positive, and easy to talk to.

We got engaged in September of 1974, when I was a senior at Brigham Young University. I was so excited that I couldn't concentrate on anything else, especially school. We set the wedding date for Friday, December 13. Because many couples had been superstitious and changed their wedding date from Friday the 13th, we were able to plan the wedding and reception without any problems, even though we only had a few months to prepare. We were married in the Salt Lake Temple for time and all eternity. Then shortly after, I was introduced to the whirlwind of show business. I will admit now that it was an overwhelming adjustment, having come from a family of four. But, I eventually got used to the lifestyle and saw the positive side of the business, the best part being the opportunity to make so many new friends around the world.

As I look back on almost 35 years of marriage, I can honestly say that I never once doubted Wayne's love for me, even when other girls were thronging to touch him and talk to him. What is even more interesting is that if anyone was a little insecure in our relationship at times, it was Wayne. Wayne never took me for granted or showed a lack of love and devotion. During the past 35 years of marriage, he has told me many times a day that he loves me and appreciates me.

Before you decide that Wayne is perfect, he'll be the first one to tell you that he isn't. I love the fact that he has an earnest, sincere, desire to be the best person that he can be. Someone asked me one weekend when we arrived in Albuquerque, New Mexico, "Do you realize how lucky you are?" Yes, I realize what a jewel I have for a husband, and I will love and cherish him eternally.